GOUPI RED HANDS
IN PARIS

GOUPI RED HANDS IN PARIS

by
PIERRE VÉRY

Translated from French by
ALAN GRIMES

Francophile Press

Copyright licensee of translation rights © 2007 Alan Grimes

The moral right of the author has been asserted.

Apart from any fair dealing for the purposes of research or private study,
or criticism or review, as permitted under the Copyright, Designs and Patents
Act 1988, this publication may only be reproduced, stored or transmitted, in
any form or by any means, with the prior permission in writing of the
publishers, or in the case of reprographic reproduction in accordance with
the terms of licences issued by the Copyright Licensing Agency. Enquiries concerning
reproduction outside those terms should be sent to the publishers.

Francophile Press

4 Harmer Lane, Cringleford
Norwich, Norfolk NR4 7RT
www.pierrevery.co.uk

ISBN 978-0955243-912

Typeset in 11pt Bembo by Troubador Publishing Ltd, Leicester, UK
www.troubador.co.uk

Elizabeth - For her continuous support

BRADFORD METROPOLITAN LIBRARIES	
B184948980	
Bertrams	07.12.07
	£6.99
SHY	

CONTENTS

Introduction ix
Acknowledgements xi

ONE	Tongking's Family	1
TWO	Sister Catherine of the Nativity	9
THREE	The Lady of the Stations	18
FOUR	Saint Agatha's Boarding House	24
FIVE	Funny Business	34
SIX	Further Funny Business	42
SEVEN	Goupi – Mousmé	48

PART TWO RED HANDS IN PARIS

EIGHT	Titmouse Private Post	71
NINE	'Mr.' Red Hands	88
TEN	The Secret of St. Agatha's	97
ELEVEN	Hand Games	116
TWELVE	'Inspector' Red Hands	124
THIRTEEN	Blood for Supper	134
FOURTEEN	Red Hands on the Eiffel Tower	149

INTRODUCTION

PIERRE VÉRY'S FRENCH WONDERLAND: POST-WAR PARIS AND THE RURAL IDYLL

Over the course of decades fictional detectives have come in many different guises : omniscient amateurs with chambers in Baker Street, hard-bitten private eyes, unassuming clergymen, comic aristocrats, psychologists haunted by their own demons, convicted burglars and even, on occasion, professional policeman. But it is the French who have distinguished themselves in choosing the most *unlikely* professions for their literary creations. Pierre Tabaret, the central protagonist of Émile Gaboriau's *L'Affaire Lerouge* (1866), arguably the first modern detective novel, is a retired pawnbroker, a contemptible trade by the standards of the day. More recently, Daniel Pennac's Benjamin Malaussène, one of the more memorable characters of the 1980's and 90's, is a fulltime scapegoat, that is, he is employed by firms such as department stores to deflect the anger of dissatisfied customers on to himself by his maladroit behaviour.

Even in the face of competition as strong as Tabaret and Maulaussène, Pierre Véry's Goupi Mains Rouges, a child of nature and poacher who doubles as gravedigger in the isolated farming community of his native Charentes, cuts an eccentric figure as an independent one-man fictional sleuth. Isolated by choice from the daily routines of his family and neighbours, he is also cut off from the world so completely that even a telephone is a daunting, newfangled luxury. The prospect of a first trip to Paris is a huge challenge for Goupi.

But it would be wrong to write him off at the outset. *Goupi Mains Rouges à Paris* first appeared in 1949, after the liberation of France and the cynical manipulation of a nation out of a charmed prewar period. It appeared twelve years after *Goupi Mains Rouges* which will have been remembered by many of the reading public, particularly as in 1943 Jacques Becker's film version appeared, with Fernand Ledoux playing a masterfully taciturn Goupi. Véry was attracted to cinema writing and impressed by Becker's *film-noir style*.

All Véry's work is marked by fantasy and paradox but in *'Goupi Red Hands à Paris'* a new element of social realism is apparent. Paris is no longer simply a charmed arena in which magical if mysterious events take place, but a sinister cityscape that contains sordid encounters. Of all Véry's works this is the most gritty.

Terry Hale
January 2007

ACKNOWLEDGEMENTS

Dr. Terry Hale, one-time director of the British Centre for Literary Translation, has continued to make available his expertise in the extensive field of French detective fiction. I am really most appreciative of this.

Emeritus Professor John W. Fletcher, formerly of the University of East Anglia, was good enough to give his professional attention to the entire script. Needless to say, the script has benefitted considerably and I am most grateful to him.

Faye Briony Pearson painted the cover illustration and has evoked skilfully the ambience of Goupi's feelings on entering the great city of madness.

Pierre Véry's son, Noël continues to work steadily to promulgate his late father's works to the largely untapped British detective fiction reading public.

Jeremy Thompson of Troubador Publishing Ltd. has again been a guide and constant help on the detail of self-publishing and Julia Fuller has been most effective in dealing with marketing matters.

Finally, the patience and support of my wife throughout the preparation of this script has to be recorded. As if that were not enough, she has passed an unrelenting eye over the whole script.

Readers having translational problems with my original text should send comments to:
alangrimesb@yahoo.co.uk
For more detailed information on other titles by this author, or on transaltors, go to:
www.troubador.co.uk and
www.pierrevery.co.uk

CHAPTER 1

TONGKING'S FAMILY

Red Hands had blood on his hand.

But instead of hiding away, he deliberately came out of the wood just as Goupi-Law was passing. He broke the breech of his gun and threw the spent cartridge case on to the road on purpose. Deliberately, to bother this old fool Goupi-Law.

Three hare's heads were hanging from his haversack, one of them still bleeding.

'They weigh a good five pounds each,' Red Hands mocked, scraping sun-dried blood from his hand.

'You know I don't enjoy being the policeman,' Law began. Red Hands exploded with laughter. 'But if I wasn't retired, I would be obliged to raise a statement from you.'

'The older you get, the dafter you become,' Red Hands replied amiably.

Poaching, this was his life! It was doubly enjoyable poaching on Goupi property. This branch of the Goupi family actually owned this land, the woods, meadows, vineyards, fields of wheat and maize, beets, horses, cows, sheep, pigs, an army of poultry, barns crammed with hay and straw, lofts laden with grain, nuts and potatoes, cellars filled with barrels and the spacious domestic quarters had a kitchen and cupboards overflowing with dripping, bacon, preserves, hams. Drawers bulged with linen and under these piles were wads of banknotes. Not to mention that clock, which made sure that time in the Goupi place was better than money – the weights and the pendulum were of gold!

The most comical feature of this was that the Goupis were unaware of it. They went on searching everywhere for this treasure which was staring them in the face. Pitiful! It was to this rogue Red Hands that the dying Goupi-Emperor had revealed the hiding place of the treasure which no-one had to touch. In turn Red Hands on his own deathbed would convey the secret to Goupi-Monsieur. But between now and then, he had the satisfaction of thumbing his nose at them.

'I've stolen three hares from you, another three', Red Hands insisted. 'What are you waiting for, to put me in clink?'

'Goupi affairs concern only the Goupis,' Law retorted. He was fuming, thinking to himself, 'the worst thing is that this bugger Red Hands may have stolen the treasure from us. How shall we know?'

'Give me a pipe, that'll be better.'

'Blackmailer,' grumbled Law, disgusted.

Red Hands coolly helped himself to half the packet of rough tobacco and then, insolently touching the peak of his cap, whistled his dog Satan and moved off.

'And to say that is the scoundrel who will one day have the pleasure of digging my grave.' Law reflected angrily.

★ ★ ★

The treasure, Red Hands really despised it! His only wealth was his memories and God knows they weren't happy.

Lison, his sister. She was so beautiful they could do no better than give her the sobriquet of Goupi-Belle. Goupi-Law had banned her marrying a lad from an orphanage because he had no prospects of an inheritance! Heartbroken, the wretched Belle had thrown herself down a well. Dead, she was even more beautiful than alive; no-one could bring themselves to believe she no longer breathed. To the extent that, to get themselves used to the idea that she was dead, really dead, they were obliged to change her name, calling her Goupi-Dead.

Thank God Red Hands was not the gravedigger in those days ... . He would have been obliged to dig hers ... .

He had however dug those of Mary, the old servant, and her son, the innocent John. John was like Red Hands himself, he had loved things for their own sake rather than for the personal pleasure of possessing them...animals, the grass in the fields, the forest with its smells and voices.

Another ghost was Goupi-Tongking the sniggerer, whose brains had been eaten away by the tropical sun. He only knew how to speak of colonial matters – Indo-China, the East, lands of colour and light – far away, overseas. Goupi-Adage had refused him his own daughter Goupi-Lily and he had become demented. His grave also Red Hands had dug ... .

And yet another ghost, one they had seen turn up one Saturday in the middle of the wine harvest, with a small girl in her arms! A slim, slant-eyed, bronze-coloured creature, in poor health and so gentle and humble, who spoke as one sings. She had just arrived from the colonies and did not know that Tongking was dead.

'My husband' she said.

Such effrontery! ... why not a black girl while he was about it?

'Married behind the Town Hall'. One of those native girls – how many had he had there? To how many had he related in his own way the history of France, lying on a mat during his four 'jungle years' as he called them?

My God! He had given this one a child! Of course, the Goupis had protested at the deception – she carried no papers to prove her statements. And the Goupis believed only in credentials, preferably stamped documents, government forms, official phrasing or rubber stamps.

They had slammed the door in her face.

Red Hands had welcomed both mother and child into

his hut in the forest. Accustomed to living on rice, he had fed them hare, wild rabbit and young partridge.

After a winter spent coughing the mother was dead – another grave to dig. And Red Hands alone with the child.

At school her companions had called her Mousmé – Goupi-Mousmé – because of the East surely? And they disliked her because she was born six thousand miles away from Charente. Her eyes had seen stars shining that they would never see. Above all and quite simply she was pretty, really pretty – a successor to the late Goupi-Belle.

One evening, returning home from the hunt, Red Hands had found a note pinned to the eiderdown on his bed:

Red Hands, forgive me. I like you very much but I am leaving. I know that this is bad but I cannot do otherwise than go. I will come back – one day.

Mousmé was then eighteen. A Tongking, who could blame her? If the Tongkings started settling in a place, the world would be upside down!

She was gone because everyone hated her, apart from Red Hands. Also, because she was feeling shut away in this cramped district. She longed for space. The light was too poor, the sun in Europe is cold and weary. In Charente there was not enough air for her to breathe.

I will come back – one day.

That was three years ago and Red Hands waited patiently for her. One day surely she would return. These Tongkings, it had always finished with their coming back. They fall on you from the sky one beautiful morning when least expected. And they say 'Hallo, Uncle. You slept well?' As though they had left the previous evening. They don't work to the same clock as others.

★ ★ ★

Red Hands was wandering back to his house.

A young lad, his nose glued to the handle bars of his dérailleur-geared bike, passed him at twenty two miles an hour. Goupi-Champ...

He was training for the Montmoreau-Mouthiers return circuit and imagined having his baton of the future winner of the Tour de France in his toolbag! The makings of a Tongking ... go!

A large clumsy lump of a man came out of the church – backwards in deference to God – it was Goupi-Beadle the sacristan. He had wrinkles on his forehead which alone made up the sign of the cross. He had just rung the Angelus. He greeted the priest, Goupi-My Brothers, who was with his second cousin Goupi-Sprinkle, the tall seminarist. Both were giving Goupi-Cruet the choirboy a lecture. They had caught him making sealing wax from the hosts!

In a field a man and woman were gathering late potatoes. The man was Goupi-Purgatory, who had the unhappy privilege of being wedded to a real shrew. She wore a wig and beneath this hairpiece her pate was as smooth as a knee; she was known as Goupi-Knee.

Goupi-Good Mark and Goupi-Hundred Lines, both primary school teachers, were discussing politics with the pharmacist Goupi-Enema.

And everywhere around were scattered Goupis – the uncountable Goupi tribe!

Goupi-Half-Wit, the local idiot, Goupi-Petticoats, a true womaniser, Goupi-Gazette the postman, Goupi-Parliament the mayor who fantasised about being elected member of parliament, Goupi-Trollop who gave herself to anyone; it was enough to raise a finger for her to hop into bed, Goupi-Dodge Death the doctor, Goupi-Post Office, the woman who was suspected of writing anonymous letters, Goupi-Will the solicitor, Goupi-Bellyful who was permanently pregnant; one child did not wait for another! Fortunately, her sister was Goupi-Angel the midwife. Goupi-Lends to God, whose motto was, 'who lends to the poor lends money to God' lived by begging. Goupi-Cinder was actually Alexander, which gives Sandy, which gives Cinder. Etc... etc...

One could go on for ever.

It was just a game. These people were not actually Goupis. Watching the lights pricked out in the dusk, Red Hands was simply amusing himself imagining that the area was populated with Goupis. He created these names to make himself smile. And he entertained himself romancing that there were only Goupis to the far end of the region — or even beyond. Nothing but Goupis in the Dordogne, Lot, in Corrèze, Creuse, in Vienne, Nièvre, Indre, in the Cher...!

By dint of dreaming, he came to a sort of thought. There are only two types of people existing in the world, whatever their names may be. There were the Goupi sort, who knew a penny is a penny, who stored and accumulated; who did not joke about principles. And there were the Tongkings, who always felt constricted, itching with curiosity, never in agreement, and with their own notion of justice and contentment... those who actually preferred to fritter their lives away.

Of course it was not that simple. Nothing is. There are mixtures, salads. Goupis who have not managed to shake off a drop of Tongking blood; this had made them do silly things. And Tongkings who had retained a little Goupi blood, which stopped their slide.

But on the whole there was truth in the idea of the Goupis and the Tongkings.

For example, Red Hands had a taste for wandering in the woods, a God-fearing horror of suffocating between four walls; even in his own shack which was open to any wind he felt in a strait-jacket. He disliked the police. He had a reputation as a sorcerer with his magic and his bewitchments for use on idiots. He had sharp eyes that he hid beneath his brows to provoke fear. He had never killed anyone with his bare hands in spite of their bad reputation.

He was artful, with an instinct for practical jokes. He had a passion for remaining poor, a supreme flaw among the Goupis. He told himself with satisfaction that he was a true Tongking.

Balanced right at the top of the Goupi family tree was Goupi-Bagman, a pedlar without hearth or home who had nevertheless given the lie to the proverb that a rolling stone gathers no moss; he had found a treasure! A Tongking from top to toe that one – the Tongking of Tongkings.

It was from him that Red Hands had inherited what was best in him!

★ ★ ★

Red Hands passed by a young girl. It was almost dark but he recognised her outline : Aimée Laprade.

She had not recognised him and stepped slightly aside.

'Good evening Miss Aimée,' he spoke to put her at ease.

'Good evening, Red Hands…'

He heard her move away. She pressed more on the ground with her right than her left foot, a sign that she was carrying quite a heavy load.

Red Hands nodded his head.

He knew the girl well. Not that they had ever had any conversations but he had seen her many times sitting at her window, had so often met her at the edge of the forest or along by the water with a book under her arm, always the same one.

Above all, Red Hands knew her father Alban Laprade the solicitor, the one christened by them Goupi-Will. A dyed in the wool Goupi, the pure juice, the essence of a Goupi.

And Aimée – a Tongking.

Red Hands was pondering 'Another one who, one of these evenings will no longer be able to stand it. Who will go off, without fuss – just like Mousmé.'

Now, it was no bundle that Aimée Laprade was carrying, it was a suitcase. She had stuffed it with a few clothes and all manner of useless objects of which she was fond.

Because that very evening, Aimée Laprade was running away from her father's house.

CHAPTER 2

SISTER CATHERINE OF THE NATIVITY

Out of sight on the edge of the undergrowth and some fifty metres from the bus stop for Poste Manquée, Aimée Laprade was waiting for the country coach – the bus as it was called – and was shivering in her beige gabardine autumn coat. And yet this early October was unusually mild.

But it was on the inside that Aimée was cold. In her ears she still had the sound of the dead leaves disturbed by each step as she hurried through the chestnut grove.

Yes, it really was from death that she was escaping – everything in this country was just dead. The twenty years that she had lived there had been twenty dead years. And as for this group of women in headscarves with shopping bags, and the men in working blue that she vaguely made out near the bus stop, they were nothing more than dead. They uttered dead words to kill time. Oh irony!

She avoided showing herself, she knew the nosiness and the whispered comments that the sight of her would not have failed to provoke.

To get on the bus, she waited until it was on the point of driving off and she remained standing near the driver, facing the front. But she felt all these looks pressing on her. Tomorrow, when they would know of her disappearance, there would be ten, twenty of them to tell Mr. Laprade...

'Your daughter took the bus from Poste Manquée to Angoulême.'

And Mr Laprade would not understand... 'I never

denied her anything ... I didn't make her angry ... she was happy ...'

The ancient servant Mélina, who had been at Aimée's birth, she would not understand either.

'... Such a reserved young lady. As a child she was afraid of the dark; she slept buried under the blankets. I had to come and uncover her .... and shy. She had a fear of strangers. It was such a song and dance just to persuade her to say 'hallo' to a stranger ...'

And Emilie Ranouilh, Mr Laprade's secretary, she would not be able to understand either. Emilie was a little more than the secretary to Alban Laprade. After ten years of widowerhood, put yourself in her place where this man was concerned. But she contented herself with her position. If she was seeking to get herself married or, at the very least, to be named in Goupi-Will's will, she conducted herself with discretion, subtlety and the tireless patience which characterised the peasant class.

'I don't understand,' she would say. 'There have never been words between Aimée and me. We got on very well.'

So – what? An unhappy affair? One knew of no romance, happy or not, in Aimée's life.

'She's absconded.' The doctor would say.

'A fanciful girl', the primary school teacher would say.

Fine words which would explain nothing.

However, as one would very much like to find reasons, one could conclude that Aimée was odd. She talked to no-one, just 'Good day' and 'Good evening', in passing. She was always into reading. Books, that's not good, that makes for fancy thoughts.

In fact Aimée did not even read!

The eternal book bound in brown that she carried on all her walks – to strike a pose and for discouraging people who had a compulsion for boring you to tears with their chatter – was a work on jurisprudence taken at random from the solicitor's library!

For her part, the young girl, if she had been obliged to

say why she was escaping, would have found it difficult.

The single word for explaining everything was 'Tongking'.

She was leaving because she was suffocating... Because she could stand it there no longer...

She had left a letter for her father on the table in her room. A note certainly better composed than that which Goupi-Mousmé had pinned to Red Hand's eiderdown three years earlier. For Aimée had taken religious studies and passed the baccalaureate. But the two letters said essentially the same thing :

'Forgive me, I am fond of you. I know that this is wrong, but I cannot do anything other than leave.'

★ ★ ★

At Angoulême station the official enquired 'A ticket for where?' And it was only then that she put the question to herself. Where indeed? She had left...To get away. She wasn't going anywhere .... She was going away.

'Paris'. The first name that came into her mind. She had never been there, she had no relative there, no acquaintance.

'What class?'

'Third'

The fast train was not leaving until thirty minutes after midnight. Three long hours in the waiting room sitting on the end of a bench. Amidst the smell of stale tobacco, red wine, food for the journey like hard-boiled eggs, cold meat, cheese, and soiled cheap clothes, sour milk, and nappies soaked in urine. In an atmosphere of weariness and sleep ...

But Aimée was exalted with the prospect of living, of existing at last. She was completely focussed on the next dawn. It would be the first sunrise that she would truly notice.

A ticket for where? For the land of the living!

★ ★ ★

In the train, Aimée occupied a place on the corridor side. She found herself opposite a man, hardly more than fiftyish, with a gentle look, a little sad and resigned, one of those who is going to die soon and knows it. Aimée wondered with what incurable disease this man was afflicted.

Several of the travellers were sleeping. Sometimes, the man under sentence of death shut his eyes just for a moment. It was not to sleep, it was to recall. He emptied the contents of his wallet on to his knees, made an inventory, tore up some papers, then scribbled some notes into a book.

'Final tidy up, last wishes', thought Aimée, which recalled her solicitor father.

On her right a foxy-looking individual was seated. He wasted no time in seeking Aimée's knee with his own. She shrank away. He had another go. Cautiously but firmly he went on with his sly sliding. Aimée could have protested, or gone out into the corridor. A strange weakness held her back. Again and again this insistent knee. The man who was soon to die was watching these manoeuvres. Finally, Aimée gave up edging away. Immobilised, pressed against his knee, she was less aware of this alien object than during the interminable minutes when he was approaching her with his reptilian caution. Then, she could not divert her thoughts. The horror of contact was less than the horror of waiting. Of course, the weasel read acquiescence in this behaviour. Soon the length of his thigh was pressed against Aimée's.

The sick-looking man pursed his lips...

He also believed that Aimée was consenting. Men understand nothing!

Suddenly Aimée recalled Madeleine Janvier, and it was like a revelation. She knew the purpose of her trip. She knew why she had gone, where, and what she had to do there.

The weasel no longer restrained his audacity, and was bold enough to slip his hand between their legs. She got up calmly.

'Excuse me sir,' she said, 'I'm getting off'.

The express was drawing into St. Pierre-des-Corps station.

The weasel courteously took Aimée's suitcase down from the rack.

'Thank you, sir.'

He gave her a smile. 'Goodbye, Miss. Good journey.'

Pathetic creep!

★ ★ ★

Still five hours to use up, five dark hours in a waiting room crossed by phantom figures as weary and smelly as those at Angoulême. But from now on nothing of this that went on around Aimée counted for her. Even the time no longer mattered.

She was going to meet up again with Madeleine Janvier.

In the train which swept her towards the final destination, Aimée had a compartment to herself. There, she indulged herself in a wild act. She very carefully sifted through the contents of her case and kept only what was essential – clothes, underwear, shoes. Everything else – knicknacks, photographs, letters, minor souvenirs, even 'Christine-France' an Alsatian doll, its hair tied with a tricolour ribbon that she had kept since childhood. All these she flung through the door. The sensual pleasure of renouncement, of deprivation! Unlimited joy was tearing open her heart and pulling her away from the earth. It was becoming smaller and smaller, became invisible, it vanished. An emotion powerful as a great eagle carried Aimée off to the heavens.

She was going to stop calling herself Aimée. Henceforth she would be Sister Catherine of the Nativity, if it was permitted. Such was the name she had chosen for herself.

She had decided to enter a convent.

Time consists simply of past and future, that is, of a double emptiness. This would fade away faced with the single reality of Eternity, which is simply the present. An everlasting adoration face to face with the Eternal Presence.

At 1.38 pm. she reached Lisieux and shortly after visited the Carmelite monastery with a group of pilgrims.

However, faced with the relics of Theresa of the Infant Jesus, she remained inattentive, almost indifferent. She could think only of this friend at the local primary school, Madeleine Janvier of Moulins village, who became a Carmelite.

At fourteen Madeleine was not yet exactly taking the road to Carmel. She ran after insolent lads by day in the woods and during the evenings in the barns. The men were saying of her, with an odd smile, that she was 'forward'.

To imagine that she was living here, immured! That she was breathing behind these stones ... Madeleine, who was no longer Madeleine. What could her saint's name be?

Madeleine had beautiful blonde hair. They had cut it when she took the veil. They would also cut Aimée's, which was jet black. She tried to imagine herself without her hair. She had a very pale, long oval face in which big sombre eyes burned.

She told herself that the white headband would set off her eyes, would make them appear darker and accentuate the fevered air which suited her so well. She soon rebuked herself for this indulgence and tried hard to think seriously of little Sister Thérèse. She asked her to sustain her first steps on the long road to faith.

Later, she was on the hillside at Terres-Noires, paying her respects at the basilica dedicated to the saint. Then she went right to the far end of the town, to breathe the air of Buissonets, that same air that the infant Thérèse Martin had breathed.

She returned slowly towards Carmel Street. 'My last steps in the secular world', she thought, and felt sorry for herself. She marvelled at the town, the very old houses, the strange sculptures, the winding streets, the little washhouses; it was all very beautiful. Rather less beautiful were the devotional articles spilling in profusion in so many shop windows. She reflected that if the good Lord had taste – and if he had not who had? – he must find all this ghastly. Seriously, what connection between these glass jewels, these inane images, and the salvation of the soul? Fleeing the shops of edifying trashy junk, she made stops in front of fashion shops, milliners and shoe-shop windows.

She went into a baker's shop but allowed herself just one item – 'my last greediness in the secular world!'

The sight of an attractive-looking young man recalled to her, by contrast, the weasel on the Bordeaux-Paris train. She shivered with revulsion so that it was disgust that carried her to the door of the convent.

A sister appeared.

'What can I do for you, Miss?

Aimée asked herself 'Am I going mad?'

She looked at the nun with some terror. An oval face like Aimée's but emaciated. Sombre eyes like Aimée's but set deeper and more feverish … Aimée had the feeling of staring at an older version of herself. In twenty years she would be like this – in a habit like this – exactly like this.

What can I do for you, Miss?' the sister repeated, surprised. Aimée felt an absurd distress and at the same time a ridiculous need to burst out laughing. Without replying she fled, panic-stricken.

Was it the word 'prison', sharply suggested to her mind by the walls of Carmel? The idea of the senior nun; this 'jailer' to whom one would have to say 'Mother Superior'. Or the terrifying image of Madeleine with head shaved – getting up in the small hours for prayers – stretched out on the floor of her cell and beating her forehead on the flagstones?

She dined in a bar near the station, nervously erupting into laughter when thinking of the nun. People were looking at her and smiling, telling themselves that this young lady had a really happy heart. She ate oysters with the appetite of a person returning from the dead. She glanced towards the manageress at her till, towards the waitresses and the customers, with the eyes of someone come back to life. Shivering from the earlier fear, she ordered pickled pork and cabbage after her omelette. 'Let's hope I don't get indigestion'. She was thinking of herself as someone who had just had a serious illness, who had escaped death.

In a nearby hôtel a porter with a limp led her to a room. It was worse than modest; the birds on the wallpaper seemed depressed at being painted in such sad colours, but Aimée felt like singing for them!

And even when she recalled the weasel on the fast train, before falling asleep, it was done without loathing this time – with a pitying smile, no more.

She dreamed of a funeral – good omen!

The following morning she lazed about in bed until midday.

At four-twenty she boarded the Cherbourg-Paris express. She had bought a novel – she who never read! A who-dunnit.

From the outset the author, a man who knew his trade and his public, entered into the fat of his subject, you could say into the red meat of it.

Someone knocked in a curious way on the office door of Mr Valletta, the magistrate.

'Come in!' The astonished magistrate said.

The dead man entered.

'Good evening,' he said, 'how are you?'

Aimée closed her eyes and pondered a moment on the sort of work she would find in Paris. She knew so little of things, you might say nothing! Not even how to type. Pooh! … . She would see.

She returned to her reading.

A strangled cry burst from the magistrate's throat.
'Well hullo, hullo,' mocked the dead man,' you recognise me!'
He sat down without ceremony on a corner of the desk.
'You see no objection to my having a fag?'

Amused, intrigued, Aimée smiled. She had had a spiritual crisis – it was gone.

Farewell – 'sister Catherine of the Nativity!'

CHAPTER 3

THE LADY OF THE STATIONS

The express drew into St Lazare station at 6.54 pm. The passengers jumped from the moving train and ran towards the barrier.

On other platforms, other travellers of all ages ran towards their trains. And a crowd of other people from the streets also charged across the hall towards these platforms and the trains.

It was rush hour when all the working commuter population is stirred into a swarm which mixes mechanic and shop assistant, Woolworth employee and insurance clerk.

At the heart of this stampede, this scramble, this disorderly procession, was Aimée, who had come from Goupi country where time moved in slow motion, where a hundred times a day one is tempted to drive people on, to push the hands of the clock, to make them move faster.

A woman in dark clothes, wearing a red and yellow armband, looked at the young lady and made a step towards her but, catching sight of a very poor woman laden with children and parcels, went to her and took charge of two parcels and a couple of children. They moved off.

With her small case in hand, Aimée stood dazed and dizzy.

A human Niagara – such was the initial image that this outrageous city threw in her face. Did everyone rush like this from dawn to dusk in Paris? For a moment she thought of some huge catastrophe: a district ablaze, revolution ... .

But she noticed a couple embracing. Then another. Then a number of others. Boys and girls in corners, against walls, against pillars. Lost in a dream of paradise they kissed, gazed at each other, smiled, hugging again, quivering with passion! Milestones of affection in this advancing tide. Aimée asked herself whether Paris was a city where half the population was devoted to running and the other half to love.

'My child ...'

She started and looked up quickly. A man dressed in navy blue was smiling at her. His beard, long but sparse, was curiously spotted with tiny red and blue ladybirds, the pattern of his tie which was showing through the scanty hair of his beard.

'This is your first visit to Paris?' She nodded. 'And no-one is meeting you?' Again a nod. 'This is a terrible city my child. Dreadfully forbidding for a young lady on her own.'

She looked at him with astonishment but without fear. This navy blue suit, the ribbon in the buttonhole, the beard which announced that he was on the wrong side of sixty... And even including the touching little ladybirds!

Suddenly panic. Mr Laprade had warned the police. They had sent a description of Aimée – he was a police inspector!

'I'm not an inspector, my dear.'

So he had the gift of reading thoughts?

'But ...Who are you, sir?'

'Come, if you will', he gave as an answer, 'as far as that poster down there, please.'

The poster was slashed with an orange and yellow band.

'Read it, my child.'

She read:

CHARITY FOR PROTECTION
OF THE YOUNG WOMAN

'Well?'

'Well, now you know who I am'. He stroked his beard

with care, not only was it sparse but it was insecurely rooted. He could scarcely touch it without bits of hair remaining between his fingers.

He pulled a red and yellow armband from his pocket and placed it for a second on his arm then put it back in his pocket:

'I am,' he said, still smoothing his beard, 'I am "The Lady of the Stations!"'

Aimée was so staggered she forgot to laugh!

'When I say that I am a lady', he corrected himself, 'that is a manner of speaking. But nevertheless you can have total confidence in me.'

He unfolded a paper.

'Do you know this weekly?'

'FORWARD. It's the Salvation Army. Yes. I know.'

'A great and splendid charity. I have the honour of belonging to it.'

He showed her a Salvation Army card carrying his photograph.

Still dragging the mother and her swarm of offspring, the woman with the red and yellow armband passed close to them.

'A colleague. We are doing our best to bring help. But there is so much poverty.' He sighed. He shook his head:

'Neither relatives nor acquaintances here, eh?'

Aimée agreed.

He sighed again. 'Believe me, I understand you, my little Germaine.'

'You're making a mistake,' she was relieved. Everything is explained she thought, it's mistaken identity.

He laughed softly.

'You are not called Germaine! Excuse me, it's an odd habit of mine, nothing nasty! I like trying to work out people's Christian names. I said to myself "this young lady has the look of someone who is called Germaine". It's a very common name in Normandy. I know four Germaines and all four are Norman'.

'How do you know I am from Normandy? She slipped in craftily.

'A little bird told me', he joked. 'And your train comes from Cherbourg… A little bird,' he continued, 'also told me here is a young lady who is a minor and who has just done something rash. Come now, don't be alarmed! An impulse – isn't that it? You'd fallen in love, eh? With someone your family disapproved of! And Papa was strict. One morning you were tired of being kept on a short rein down there at home near Caen or Vire, eh?… You wanted to live your life, trying your luck in the capital, right? Taking advantage of your youth, eh, little butterfly? Your story is the story of many others. Come on now.' He became serious. 'I hope at any rate that you have not … done anything silly? You understand me?'

She laughed. She was no longer apprehensive.

'Although I've just come from Normandy, I'm no more Norman than I'm Germaine! And I did not leave one morning, but one evening. My father was not strict; he did not keep me on a short rein. I'm not in love with any man. I have listened to none of them.'

'But they wanted to impose someone on you?'

'Wrong again. Your little bird misinformed you.'

He was not offended.

'Anyway,' he said sadly, 'it did not lie to me in telling me that you ran away from the parental home … . Why did you do that?'

She did not speak.

'Why, my child?'

She made a vague gesture, 'I can't explain it to you.'

'Yes…It is often the most important things that one has the most trouble defining. But believe me, I understand you!'

'How could you? There are times when I no longer understand myself!'

'Because you cannot stand back. At sixty-two years of

age, one has the necessary distance. Come my dear. We're going to put a little order into all that.'

'But I haven't the least wish to go to the Salvation Army! I'm not destitute.'

'Who spoke of that? I am going to introduce you to my sister. She spends her life helping young girls in your situation. She will counsel you, direct you, she will open doors for you.'

Aimée hesitated.

He pointed out to her a man strolling around. 'Police inspector.'

That decided it. She let him take her case and they began to move off.

'Actually,' he said briskly, 'forgive me, I forgot to introduce myself. I'm Mr Blue. Hippolyte Blue.'

Why – with what remained of her mistrust – instead of replying 'Aimée Laprade', did she borrow the name of that old friend become Carmelite.

'My name is Madeleine Janvier.'

'That doesn't suit you, Madeleine.' Then, 'You see no objection to my having a little puff?'

'Ah!' reflected Aimée, amused, 'just the words of the dead man in the whodunnit.'

'Ah, well, good Madeleine, forward,' said Mr Blue with gusto. He laughed. 'An old habit, FORWARD, that's our newspaper.' He blew a puff of smoke voluptuously. 'I'm taking you to the foot of the Eiffel Tower.'

A moment later they set off down Avenue Charles-Floquet .

'Stop!' he said shortly after. They were in front of a quaint, crumbling, single-storied old house. An erection out of tune with the times, ripe for demolition, and which appeared more miserable still to be slotted between two tall freestone buildings. One had the feeling that the tenants of this dump must be ashamed of breathing the superior air which bathed this corner of Paris – air for wealthy people which was carefully recharged with oxygen every night from the trees of Champ-de Mars!

Over the door there was this inscription:

SAINT AGATHA INSTITUTION
Protection of the Young Woman

'Go in, dear,' said Mr Blue, 'and consider yourself at home.'

CHAPTER 4

SAINT AGATHA'S BOARDING HOUSE

Four girls of twenty to twenty five years, powerfully built like barges, were waxing the lobby floor.

Aimée took them for servants.

'Your colleagues,' said Mr Blue. And to the girls he said. 'A new arrival!'

Aimée looked at them with amazement – two red apples for cheeks, huge paws, breasts which evoked milching cows, and rumps like mares, which strained the fabric of their dresses to breaking point.

Aimée picked up her case and was going off when an astonishing apparition nailed her to the spot.

A Hercules in petticoats, a hussar in drag was approaching her, a giantess, magnificent as a Michelangelo statue. And in front of her, fluttering like doves, two wonderful fat white hands – real bishop's hands – but which one guessed were capable of battering a bull to death or strangling a python! A thin moustache streaked her face, falling on each side of her mouth like a Tartar. Stuck between the lips was a cigar.

Aimée gazed at this extraordinary woman with trepidation.

'Mrs. Agatha Blue, my sister,' said Mr Blue. And to Mrs. Blue, 'Miss Madeleine Janvier, a new member of some quality.'

'You're impossible, Hippolyte!' Mrs. Blue shouted. She included Aimée as witness.

'My brother must have been a good Samaritan in another

life! Of course, I'm delighted to see you, but the boarding house is going to close down. I gave my last class this afternoon.'

Again, to her brother, 'you know very well that we are signing the sale contract tomorrow with Mr Bertrand.'

'Tomorrow is far away, little sister!' Mr Blue answered.

'What! Don't we have a meeting tomorrow with him?'

'Who knows?' replied Mr Blue.

'How do you mean "who knows?" '

'The future belongs to God,' the brother spoke with piety, 'Bertrand may die tonight.'

'And why do you wish that he dies tonight?'

'I didn't say that I wished it. I say that it is in the order of possible things. People die every night.'

Mrs. Blue shrugged her shoulders.

'I'm sorry,' said Aimée, 'I wouldn't want to trouble you.'

'Not at all, young lady. Don't think of it,' murmured Mrs. Blue. 'Come. We are going to further our acquaintance. Look, here in the classroom, for example.'

She indicated a room and with a finger pushed Aimée, whose apprehension turned into amazement.

The room did not recall anything of a classroom. It had no benches, desks nor a rostrum, but armchairs approximating to Louis XVI style and hung with imitation Liberty prints. On the walls there were no blackboards, maps, natural history diagrams nor comparative weights and measures charts, but cheap reproductions in delicate, erotic brushwork of minor anonymous masters of the XVIII century.

'This Mr Bertrand,' Mrs. Blue was meanwhile explaining, 'wants to open a florist here. He's right, he'll make a mint of money. Mark you, it isn't that in this area they like flowers more than elsewhere. But the people have more means.'

Mr Blue showed his beard in the doorway.

'This young lady knows no-one in Paris and she is in a difficult position.' He was tearful. 'I could not have left on the pavement this bird fallen from the nest'.

He withdrew.

'I've come from Lisieux,' Aimée responded to the silent quizzing of Mrs. Blue. 'I've left the Carmelite convent. My father runs a large fishery firm in Arcachon.'

She poured all this nonsense out and, at the same time told herself, 'I'm ridiculous. She is going to ask me for my identity papers and will see very well that...' But the tangle of lies went on rolling from her mouth and she marvelled at herself to see with what ease one could invent. 'I ought to have written novels!'

And then, all this had such small importance; she was going to leave. There was no question that she would stay, even for one day, in this crazy boarding house.

She continued to play out her comedy :

'My father wanted me to make a marriage of convenience, for the benefit of his business, you know, Madame? With a boy I didn't love ... I preferred the convent. Only I had no vocation ... Then.'

'But of course!' Mrs. Blue was indulgent. 'All that is so clear.'

She did not ask to see the identity papers, and confined herself to sighing :

'Parents frequently have the fault of forgetting that they have been young.'

She opened a case filled with cigarettes ranging from Gauloises to Abdullahs, via American and English.

'Help yourself! ... You're not at Carmel here.'

'Thank you Madam. I don't smoke.'

'Believe me my girl, I'm not seeking to push you into vice,' Mrs. Blue was smiling. 'But I'm of the view that some small weaknesses have their uses. Could this be just to allow for making sacrifices when the time comes and the arteries harden and the liver gets congested? ... Personally, I'm waiting for sixty or so to renounce the cigar and to go into my second childhood!'

She became serious again.

'Tomorrow I will see what I can do for you. In the

meantime, go and sort out your things, and eat and sleep, without worries. I am going to take you to the Marys' dormitory. Because you, you are a Mary! No need to look at you twice...!'

'A Mary?'

'You who have just left the convent, surely you know that passage in the Gospel where you see Martha doing the housework and complaining how her sister Mary, seated at Jesus's feet, does nothing. Well, I divide women into two categories, those who are born to be served and those who are meant to serve. The Marys and the Marthas. I place the Marthas as general servants; the Marys, I take care of their future.'

She led Aimée through narrow rooms with low ceilings into a slightly larger room. Four single beds were accommodated there with difficulty.

'The Saint Mary dormitory,' she announced.

On a bedside table was a slim volume – Coleridge's *The Rime of the Ancient Mariner*.

'You've told me you have 'A' levels. Do you know English?'

'A little.'

Mrs. Blue opened the book and pointed out a passage. 'Read.'

Aimée, taken aback, read out:

Water, water, everywhere,
Nor any drop to drink
The very deep did rot : O Christ!
That ever this should be!

'Not bad,' said Mrs. Blue, 'but your "Th" is not up to scratch, my pet. She carried on, oddly. 'Are you anti-military? I mean to say, have you got something against officers in general and colonels in particular? I'm very involved with an English colonel ... A gorgeous creature ... But I'm not even giving you time to settle in. We'll talk about all this...'

She tested a bed:

'The mattress is excellent. I hope you'll sleep well. You will have just one room mate – Agnès Duffeteaux of Aubusson, a charming little thing. You two are going to become friends.'

She curled her moustache and then, in the same tone of voice, smiling : 'Tomorrow, my dear "Madeleine" you will tell me your real name if you wish, who your real father is, what his real job is and where he actually works. And what the true reasons are which pushed you into run away!'

Aimée had gone pale, blushed, tears welled up and she wanted to confess everything.

'Shh …' Mrs. Blue said. 'No hurry. You carry on being "Madeleine Janvier" for this evening, it's as good a name as any other. Come, I'm going to introduce you to Agnès.'

Closing the dormitory door again, she whispered mischievously,

'The Marthas' room…The Marys' room … The Institute of Saint Agatha. You'll not be too much of a fish out of water… For someone who left a convent!'

By dint of the surprises, Aimée's ability for astonishment was blunted.

An unknown old man, losing his hair like a tired feather duster, who introduces himself as the 'Lady of the Stations' and who approaches you to take you to an unbelievable boarding house – which must close down the next day! – whose manageress wears a moustache, smokes, and looks like a man, guesses that you have lied to her but shows no hurry to know the truth, gives you a passage of Coleridge to read, is concerned to know if you are anti-military and if you have anything against colonels in the British Army…

Paris really was a strange city!

In a corridor they passed a youth with hair and jacket too long and trousers too short. He was humming *Danse Macabre*.

'It's crazy the snoring noise these skeletons make,' he announced to Mrs. Blue. 'I never would have believed that one was able to find so many topics for laughter in a cemetery.'

'It's nothing,' said Mrs. Blue, 'he's my son. Laziness personified. I love him. He's preparing a book, well, an album rather. Illustrations with captions, called *Joys from the Beyond*.

★ ★ ★

Meanwhile, Hippolyte Blue was sipping an aperitif on the terrace of a café near Montparnasse station. He was irritated, he had left his copy of FORWARD at Saint Agatha's. Just at that moment, an elderly woman in Salvation Army uniform had come to offer this weekly to customers. However, the customers were composed mainly of street girls and handsome men attached to their wealth.

'You wouldn't have rather *La Vie Parisienne*?' One of them asked wittily.

'I'm afraid not. I can only offer you Eternal Life,' the old lady replied kindly.

Mr Blue called her and held out twenty francs.

'It's Providence which sends you!' He commented amiably. 'Moreover,' he added even more aimiably,' wherever you go it's always Providence that sends you.'

Shortly afterwards, he went into the station. Just in time to observe the stream of travellers disembarking from the Brest express.

After some minutes he approached a frightened young girl, a silly type with a scared, fearful look on her face. He launched into the little talk he had held with Aimée at St. Lazare station.

'You're called Yvonne, aren't you? You have the look of someone who is called Yvonne. Come on, I understand you. Father was strict; he held you on a tight rein... You wanted to come to live your life in Paris, didn't you, little butterfly? I hope at least you haven't done anything foolish?'

He led her up to the red and yellow poster on 'Charity for the Protection of the Young Woman'. He showed the weekly FORWARD … He pulled out his Salvation Army membership card, and again put on his red and yellow armband. He carefully stroked his inadequately planted beard.

'I am the "Lady of the Railway Stations" and I am going to introduce you to my sister. She will open doors for you.'

Suddenly he remembered that Saint Agatha's was going to close; that no later than tomorrow the sale contract with Mr Bertrand was going to be signed. If he brought back a new one, especially this prospective servant, a Martha, another useless mouth to feed, Mrs. Blue would get angry.

'I have to make a telephone call,' he said. 'Wait here for me, and don't move. As long as you are under the protection of this poster, you will not run into trouble.'

And he made off to take the Metro.

As he was going back into St. Agatha's, Mrs. Blue was leaving it.

'I'm going to my loves.'

'Give them my regards,' he replied.

On their beds in the Marys' dormitory, Aimée and Agnès Duffeteaux were chatting.

Agnès was very different from the four girls Aimée had surprised busily waxing the floorboards. Puny, with a shifty eye, a constipated look, and a nose like an eagle's beak over the two thin red lines of her lips.

Right away, Aimée had felt an antipathy based on disgust for Agnès. One of the latter's first confidences had been that her periods were irregular and painful. But in her unsettled state Aimée felt the need to speak to someone and conversation was not possible with the Marthas. In any case, they were already sleeping and all four were heard snoring the other side of the partition.

Two metallic objects clinked against each other.

'That's Mr Blue in his dark room,' said Agnès.

Mr Blue had in fact exchanged his navy blue suit for one of violet velvet that he particularly cared for. He was developing negatives.

'He'll certainly ask to photograph you tomorrow! We've all been done! Photography is his thing.'

The two young ladies began to show each other their stockings, their bras, their girdles and slips, and had exchanged comments on other frivolities – the quality, reliability, price, and not forgetting the make and shade of powder and lipstick.

'My father is deputy director of a bank in Aubusson,' Agnès now said. 'He insisted I make my career in banking and me, I have a musician's vocation. So I left...'

Aimée in turn spoke of her solicitor father. On this matter she was amazed that Mrs. Blue had so easily guessed that she had lied to her.

'Ah!', said Agnès, 'we all lie to her the first day.'

In this way Aimée learned that all the boarders at St Agatha's were, like herself, at odds with the paternal home.

Missing Persons in effect!

For some, it was chance that had led them to the *Protection of the Young Woman*. For others an advertisement had come to their notice. But the majority Mr Blue had 'saved', or perhaps better to say 'netted' in a railway station, on their arrival.

'Why does Mrs. Blue welcome girls who have run away from their parents home?'

'Because St. Agatha's is a charity organisation, silly! Without it what would you do? You ask such questions... !'

She made a jackknife dive under the blankets.

'Excuse me for turning my back on you. I can't sleep on my left side, I hear my heart beating and it gives me palpitations.' She yawned. 'We went to the pictures. My eyes sting.'

'You ... You go to the pictures?' Aimée could not believe it.

'So what?' You think you're in a convent?'

Aimée smiled and made no reply.

Two hours later Agnès, although she had said she was weary, was still awake.

She heard Mrs. Blue returning.

Stealthily Agnès took Aimée's handbag, the latter was asleep, and left the dormitory.

She found Mrs. Blue in the pantry, busily opening oysters. She had already laid out some salami, Camembert and a bottle of white Moselle on a table. Mrs. Blue, who enjoyed at all times an appetite in keeping with her size, was fond of these little suppers. She treated herself to them whilst reading the first scrap of newspaper that came to hand. It mattered little if it was a week old and had served to wrap groceries.

'You've come to have a bite, Agnès, my pet?'

Agnès shook her head. She had heartburn. An ulcer had been predicted and she had to take care.

She handed Aimée's handbag to Mrs. Blue

'Her name is Laprade. Her father is a solicitor near Angoulême.'

Mrs. Blue gave a glance at the papers of the new arrival only for the sake of appearances.

Agnès smiled to herself; Mrs. Blue smelled of 'Russian Leather'. However, Mrs. Blue never used perfume. She thought, 'You are coming back from your loves' place'. For Mrs. Blue's lover had a lively taste for perfume, and especially 'Russian Leather'. Agnès knew this.

Mrs. Blue gave back the bag.

'Solicitor, that's a fine profession,' she remarked dreamily.

Agnès gave her a detailed summary of her conversation with Aimée; whom she described as 'good but oafish'.

'Perfect, dear. Put the handbag back where it was and go to sleep.'

In the corridor, Agnès passed Hippolyte Blue, gorgeous as a cardinal in a purple dressing-gown.

'Interesting, the new arrival,' Mrs. Blue remarked to

him. 'she's the daughter of a solicitor from the south-west. You got it right for once.'

Hippolyte did not react to this provocative comment; he seemed preoccupied.

'I can't get off to sleep. You wouldn't have any pills? I'm tense, distressed...'

'If you hadn't stuffed yourself with coffee!' Mrs. Blue grumbled. 'Eat a dozen oysters with me. For settling the nerves, there's nothing like filling the stomach.'

'It isn't the coffee,' said Mr. Blue. He considered the oysters, they were appetising.

'All the same it's cruel eating these little creatures alive,' he said sitting down. He took one and carefully let a drop of vinegar fall onto the lip; it retracted. 'I wonder whether it suffers,' he spoke again, swallowing the oyster.

Then, 'No, it's not the coffee which gives me anguish.'

He buttered a slice of bread.

'It's because I'm thinking of a crime.'

'What!'

'Listen to me, little sister.'

He swallowed a second oyster

'I have the conviction that tonight, or tomorrow morning at the latest, a crime is to be perpetrated, on the third floor of 58 rue Lepic! Third floor, door on the right,' he specified as he poured himself a drink.

'Come on! Now you're becoming clairvoyant Hippolyte? You are getting express letters from the Beyond...?'

'It's not spiritualism... It's reasoning, Agatha. It's deduction!'

'Ah, really? ... And according to you, who is going to be murdered?'

'Mr. Bertrand of course!'

CHAPTER 5

FUNNY BUSINESS

'So? ... I am clairvoyant? I get express letters from the Beyond? ...'

Mr Blue, in the morning room, flourished the newspapers under the eyes of his dismayed sister.

CRIME OR SUICIDE?...

All the morning papers, in a paragraph composed with identical format (police communiqué), announced a mysterious death occurring during the night, on the third floor of 58 rue Lepic.

Third floor, door on the right!

Returning home at around one in the morning after an evening with friends, Mrs Lucie Bertrand had found, with a horror one can imagine, her husband Charles Bertrand in the dining room, hanging from one of the hooks holding the rail of the double curtains. An upturned chair was beneath the body. According to the forensic pathologist, death had occurred at around midnight.

That's to say that at the time when Hippolyte Blue, sampling the oysters and the Moselle wine in the pantry at St. Agatha's, was prophesying in front of his sister that someone would murder Bertrand during the night, Bertrand had already been dead for two hours! This Bertrand, who wanted to set up a flower shop and to whom the Blues had to surrender the lease the following day!

'If you weren't so idle,' said Mrs. Blue, 'I'd swear that it was you that killed him. After all, perhaps it is you. You say you spent three hours in your dark room, developing negatives. Nothing proves it!'

'And you,' he replied, 'what proof that you really went to your loves?'

They stopped this foolish game.

'I can tell you now,' Mrs. Blue continued, 'I too was expecting a misfortune.'

'This is becoming mad,' Mr Blue groaned.

It was nine o' clock in the morning.

The boarding house was resonating with comings and goings, scrapings, jarring of furniture being moved, noises of water flushing. The Marthas were doing the housework, for the last time they believed. St. Agatha's was about to close and they were going to find themselves on the street.

Aimée and Agnès were chatting in the Marys' dormitory. The cleaning did not concern them.

They heard Mrs. Blue slapping her beautiful white hands together.

'Class', said Agnès, 'but not for us. It's for the thickheads! All the same you can go there. It's worth a look.'

'Girls', Mrs. Blue declared as Aimée went into the morning room with the erotic engravings. 'I have to tell you a very sad piece of news. Mr Bertrand, who was to set up a flower shop here, died last night. It is therefore likely that the sale will not take place and that St. Agatha's boarding house will carry on.'

The four "pupils" considered this with happy faces. This sad news was the best ever for them!

'I'm taking advantage of the occasion, girls,' continued Mrs. Blue in the tone of a Mother Superior, 'to tell you that I am not praising you. I had dreamt of making you understand that women's hands are not meant for work but for wearing jewellery and being kissed. For knotting the tie of a loved one. For stroking the hair of small adorable children. Alas! Not everyone can aspire to the legendary metamorphosis of Cinderella. It's a question of bigness, one must have small feet. This is not your situation.'

The four girls wisely kept their hands crossed on their knees.

They were lusty "flowers of the field". They smelled of hay and milk. Their uncomfortable deportment and dumb expressions testified that they were born for farm and stable work, huge piles of laundry and everlasting cleaning. Not for holding a rank in society and excelling with diversions of the mind.

They were listening blissfully and not understanding a word. They loved and admired Mrs. Agatha; she was so good and spoke so well. The only consequence of this allusion to their feet was to raise in their minds the notion of sweating. For their feet sweated a good deal. Their armpits too.

'At any rate,' continued Mrs. Blue, 'I would have wished to give you a crumb of instruction.'

She leafed through some school notebooks and shook her head sadly.

'You know nothing and will never know anything...'

At that moment Mr. Blue came in with a strange and agitated air.

'Two gentlemen from the police have just arrived.' He added in a murmur, 'I believe it's best to tell them everything!'

Mrs. Blue agreed with a nod of her head. Dismissing the girls to their household chores and Aimée to the Marys' dormitory, she received the police inspectors. They had come about Bertrand.

'There is a curse on St. Agatha's!' Mr. Blue hastened to throw in and, as the word 'curse' brought a smile to the inspector's lips, he took from his pocket a piece of paper carrying some names and dates.

'I have prepared this for your benefit. You will judge for yourselves, gentlemen.'

He assumed a grave voice to make the following statement:

'Four years ago a French-naturalised Belgian, Joseph

Maertens, wanted to buy back our lease to open an art gallery here. A week before signing contracts, he was run over in rue de Miromesnil by a lorry, and died later in hospital from his wounds.'

'So what?'

'Yes, I know, these things happen, but wait. Because of the death the sale naturally didn't go through. One year later a woman, Jeanne Roussignac, began talks with us. She wanted to set up a shop selling fish and exotic birds. We agreed a price. Eighteen days before signing the agreement they found the old girl in her flat on rue le Goff, asphyxiated by the fumes of a stove. The inquest concluded it was an accident. Two of them… ! You will tell me that more than one woman asphyxiates herself by a stove. But hang on! Two years ago a certain Mr Gallant wanted to take up our lease to open here one of those studios where people come to hear songs or music recorded on discs, in automatic machines.'

'Gallant? That name rings a bell,' the inspector said.

'Of course!' Mr Blue exclaimed. 'He was assassinated! Stabbed like a pig, and robbed one night in the rue de l'Abbé-de-l'Epée. They arrested two ex-convicts who confessed to several murders, but not to that one. However, one crime more or less couldn't actually make much difference in their case.'

'You have servants.' The inspector burst out laughing. 'If it wasn't them? ...'

'Let's suppose,' said Mr. Blue. 'And three, anyway ... But that's not all. Last year someone called Berthault wanted to set up a shop here for selling fancy dogs. Do you know what became of him, Berthault? He went off his head. They had to lock him up. 'That's four! ... And now Bertrand!'

The two policemen regarded each other, slowly taking in these bizarre statements.

Maertens, Roussignac, Gallant, Berthault, and now Bertrand!

One road victim, one asphyxiation, one assassination, one mad and now, a hanged man.

But there was something perhaps stranger still than this weird series of dramas. It was that nothing in this house suggested the idea of tragedy. On the contrary. These charmingly erotic engravings. This drivelling sexagenarian with the see-through beard. This butch woman who stroked her Gengis Khan moustache and smoked cigars. How could you take the crimes seriously in such a laughable setting?

The telephone rang, making everyone jump.

'May I?' Mrs. Blue took the receiver.

'Hallo? ... Yes, this is St. Agatha's boarding house. The Protection of the Young Woman. Absolutely...
A housemaid? ... But of course, Madam. What did you say? It's a workhorse that you should have?' She smiled. 'You've come to the right place. Work-horses. I've got four at the moment. Percheron breed. One moment, I'm getting a pencil to take your address.'

She wrote: Mrs. Delaure, 18 rue de l'Assomption, sixth floor. 'Perfect. I'll come and see you myself tomorrow, to introduce the girl, and we will agree on the wages. Understood, Madam. Till tomorrow.'

Even this conversation underlined the ridiculous side of the business. The incredible aspect of the matter. A road victim, a housemaid, an asphyxiation, a housemaid, an assassination, a housemaid, a madman, a hanging ... Two maids of all work.

How could you envisage, without bursting out laughing, an implausible killer, undeterred at any price from preventing the sale of this little employment agency?

'Of course,' said Mr. Blue. 'And yet ...'

'Even if it was a question of a lunatic, it would be ... it would be weirder than anything.'

'Of course,' repeated Blue. He also repeated 'and yet.'

It was on the basis of past events that he had deduced the death of Bertrand. If the four earlier 'accidents' had really been fortuitous, there was not one chance in a million that things would repeat themselves a fifth time.

'On the other hand,' Mr. Blue was thinking, 'if the first four "accidents" had not been accidents but crimes then, inevitably, these four crimes will be followed by a fifth. The next victim will be Bertrand.'

And they had found Bertrand hanged from a curtain rail. Hanged — less than twenty-four hours before signing the deeds.

Suddenly, Gérard Blue came into the room, bursting out happily :

'I'm into skeletons up to my neck.' He noticed the policemen. 'Oh! I beg your pardon.'

'Stay, stay,' one of the inspectors quickly replied. 'We are in skeletons up to our necks too, would you believe…'

He placed himself between Gérard and the door.

'Explain yourself, young man.'

It was Mrs. Blue who explained. The drawing book. Tales from cemeteries. Amusing tales.

Funny idea!

'I'll tell you the latest,' said Gérard. 'It's in the satirical category. "*Two skeletons are strolling in the cemetery. They pass a third. They greet him formally, saying "Good day doctor" with great respect!*'

'Aha, what then?' One policeman said.

'Ah well, but … That's all.'

'Aha … And … We must laugh?'

'It's not compulsory,' replied Gérard and took himself off.

Another interlude, not exactly of the sort to contribute to a climate of fear. The inspectors indicated their wish to look around.

'Don't bother coming with us. We are going to come and go without disturbing you. A matter of getting ourselves into the feel of things.'

The feel of things! It dogged them throughout their investigations.

In a morning room Mr. Blue was photographing

Aimée – in a coat, without a coat, hair brushed, hair loose, standing, sitting...

Photography – his passion!

In the Marys' dormitory, Agnès was near an open window drying the varnish she had just put on her nails.

Mrs. Blue, in the Marthas' dormitory, had assembled the four work-horses.

'Girls, they are asking for a housemaid for a middle-class home, 18 rue de l'Assomption in the XVI district. There is a couple, an old lady, a little boy two and a half years old, a girl five years old and a boy of thirteen. The flat has seven rooms as well as storerooms in the cellar. That's telling you it's a considerable domestic service!'

The four girls put up their hands with enthusiasm.

Polishing, scraping, furbishing – this was their recreation. A packet of steel wool was the most beautiful present one could offer them!

'Since you have all volunteered, I'm going to choose by seniority,' Mrs. Blue decided, 'It will be you Emma. You know our rules. You've been here three weeks. Twenty-one days at 200 francs for board. You owe me 4,200 francs. At the beginning I will draw your wages and deduct 1,050 francs every month. In four months we will be all square. I take no profit. I content myself with getting back my advances. St. Agatha's is not a commercial enterprise, it is a charitable organisation. All I ask of you, my girl, is to do the institution honour. Morality and honesty.

'You will have only compliments, Madam.' Emma babbled.

She was overcome with pride. Daughter of Normandy farmers, her expected future had been to milk the cows, make hay and gather apples in the Condé-sur-Noireau region. To sleep in a large communal room bathed in an invigorating smell of Camembert and cider. And she had risen to the honour of service in a middle-class home. Made for guarding cows in Paradise, she aspired to washing dishes.

She aspired to talking in the third person: 'Madam asked me to tell Sir that Madam has gone to the hairdressers.' Even to the children she would speak in the third person: 'Master Louis Hulbert has soiled his rompers again.' What bliss! One worry was the young gentleman of thirteen. He would certainly seek to catch a glimpse of Emma's breasts, without seeming to, when she would be waxing the parquet floor, or mopping the tiles. Perhaps he would even ask her to show them to him one evening when Sir and Madam were at the theatre. If she refused he would say she had tried on Madam's stockings or underwear. This would be rather delicate as a situation.

Then her thoughts drifted. She told herself that there would certainly be a vacuum cleaner in this middle-class house. To operate a vacuum cleaner!

For her it was a little like driving a Rolls Royce!

CHAPTER 6

FURTHER FUNNY BUSINESS

I fear thee, Ancient Mariner
I fear thy skinny hand!

At the moment in the Marys' dormitory Mrs. Blue was making Agnès Duffeteaux read from Coleridge.

Her eyes closed, she was gently nodding her head in time with the poem, spoken in a slow and deep voice by the daughter of the deputy bank director in Aubusson:

I fear thee and thy glittering eye
And thy skinny hand so brown!

'Your pronunciation has improved but your "th" is still not perfect, my pet.' Mrs. Blue spoke.

Emma passed in the corridor, whistling. The thought of the middle-class house in the XVI district brought to her lips the trills of a nightingale.

'They whistle in stables,' thundered Mrs. Blue, 'but in middle-class houses, they don't whistle. Since this is so, you will not go to rue de l'Assomption, Emma. Charlotte will go. Carry on Agnès.'

Agnès went on:

Alone, alone, all, all alone
Alone on a wide, wide sea! …

'Lord, how marvellous!' Mrs. Blue murmured. 'English is the queen of languages, after Greek.' She continued. 'Speaking of English, I intend to get you to make the acquaintance of an English officer.'

'A lieutenant?'

'Better than that. A colonel.'

'Ah!' said Agnès, disappointed, 'so... He's old?'

'Little fool! ... He's over the recruiting board's age limit if that's what you mean to say. But he's quite someone. Former student at Oxford ... He won his pips in the Indian Army. He's a Sir! He has access to Court. Suppose you marry him? Do you see yourself in English royal circles?'

Impressed, Agnès let her head fall on Mrs. Blue's sturdy shoulder. After a silence Agnes murmured:

'Last night, Janine and Andréa went out through the window, the pair of them. They stayed out at least two hours...'

'They wear their hearts on their sleeves,' said Mrs. Blue, 'they will lose them more than once. Anyway, it's all they ask.'

'While they were out,' continued Agnès, 'Emma was stuffing herself with buttered toast in the kitchen.'

'She's not a Norman for nothing!' Mrs. Blue spoke indulgently. 'what else my little viper...?'

'Lucienne got a postcard this morning from her part of the world. Signed... "Your affectionate friend", James.'

This sneaky tittle-tattle was interrupted by the entry of the inspectors.

'It's for a piece of information,' one of them said. 'Oh, a detail ... A small thing ... the penalty deposits?'

'Penalty deposits?'

'Well yes, the penalty deposits... You've cashed them?'

It is well known that when an agreement concerned with a transfer of funds is arrived at, the prospective buyer places a deposit proportional to the sum involved into the hands of a businessman. This is the penalty deposit. Should the arrangement not go through, that is, should the option not be taken up, thus annulling the transaction, common practice requires that the penalty sum remains in the vendor's hands as a form of compensation.

'Naturally, yes, I cashed the deposits,' said Mrs. Blue.

'And you have returned them?'

'I didn't have to do that. Maertens, Emilie Roussignac and Gallant had no heirs. Berthault had signed with his wife and she had turned down buying St. Agatha's. If Mrs. Bertrand renounces opening her flower shop, the deposit will stay with me. That's normal!'

'Absolutely normal,' the inspector said sharply. 'And... these deposits come to how much altogether?'

Mrs. Blue went to fetch a file.

'Maertens, 20,000; Emilie Roussignac, 25,000; Gallant the same, 25,000; Berthault, 30,000; Bertrand, 40,000. Total, 140,000.'

'Well, well, 140,000 francs ... That makes a noise when it drops!'

'You don't imagine that my brother or I killed five people for 140,000 francs? Twenty-eight thousand per head – cheap at the price!' joked Mrs. Blue.

'People have often killed for less.' The inspector spoke idly.

At which point the telephone rang.

The call was from the CID. The Bertrand case was solved. More precisely, there was no Bertrand case; death was by suicide.

A letter in his own hand, dated and signed, showed his intention of ending his own life and the reasons for this. For some time Bertrand was prone to spasms of spitting small amounts of blood. He had been to the doctor who had asked for an X-ray.

'It's nothing,' he had said later. 'Next to nothing, an old bronchitis which has left small lesions. Take a cough syrup. Try to smoke less.'

'But I don't smoke, doctor.'

'Then just the cough syrup.'

Bertrand had not been convinced. Even less so as the manner was frivolous and the words too reassuring.

'My lungs must be affected,' was what he told himself.

He went off to see a young houseman of his acquaintance, and tried subterfuge.

'I'm worried. I have a friend who isn't well. I wouldn't be surprised if it's tuberculosis. Perhaps he should go to the mountains? I've brought you his X-ray.'

The doctor had a quick look at the negative.

'Nothing to do with tuberculosis.'

A smile appeared on Bernard's face, he was reassured … But his smile froze.

'Your friend is done for!' The intern was saying.

'What?'

'Cancer'.

'Eh?'

'Well, yes. Lung cancer. See that blot there. He spits blood, doesn't he? Look at these spots along the tracheal artery. Ganglia.'

Bertrand looked. He looked at this dismal dotted line – the itinerary of death on the move.

'Is it operable?'

'No.'

'And giving him radiotherapy?'

The doctor simply shrugged his shoulders.

'He has...

How long?' Bertrand had murmured.

'It's well established, very advanced. He can hold on for four, five months. The ganglia will press on to his trachea and slowly plug it, you understand? He will die of suffocation. It's a nasty death.'

Bertrand went home.

To put up with unspeakable suffering, to give his wife mental torture. And all that for, eventually, at the end of four to five months… . Better to finish it quickly.

In a final gesture of tenderness, he renewed the water in her flowers. They were in all the rooms. Flowers were her passion. Then he had passed a rope around a hook; he had made a slip knot…

'Excuse us, Mrs. Blue.' One of the inspectors spoke, somewhat upset as he rose.

Maertens, Roussignac, Gallant, Berthault, Bertrand... accidents... Nothing more.

The fault of bad luck…!

Not the shadow of a crime there.

'Our apologies again for troubling you, Madam. See you again.'

'See you again, gentlemen.'

On the doorstep the inspectors passed a dandy of around thirty years, swaying and dancing like a spray of flowers.

He was the music teacher. This artist was called René de Fouques.

★ ★ ★

Aimée almost laughed in Mrs. Blue's face when the latter said to her: 'Mr de Fouques is from a very ancient family. He was at the Crusades – through his ancestors.'

René de Fouques was reminiscent of a precious and crumbling object; one hesitated before shaking hands, fearful of crushing his fingers. No hair on his face; not even down. A smooth and waxen face, with the look of an angel. Silky, blond hair. A melodious voice. René de Fouques, perfumed with 'Russian Leather', evoked a scatterbrained sparrow who had perched on the ancient heraldic tree of the Counts Fouques.

To think that he was the last descendant of a line of bearded rogues, hairy giants, ever ready to clash swords, to disembowel, to do battle in order to sew together for France a rich mantle of history with great and glittering deeds.

But it is true that in his own way René de Fouques had accomplished a labour of Hercules, before which a number of his ancestors would have recoiled.

René de Fouques was not simply the music teacher at St. Agatha's.

He was also Mrs. Blue's lover!

* * *

While René was closeting himself in the music room with Agnes, Mrs. Blue in the Marys' dormitory was asking: 'Tell me a little about your father?'

Aimée blushed; the moment had come to tell the truth. With some relief she saw Gérard Blue coming in.

'Mother, I've just found another good joke for my "*Joys of the Beyond*". This time it's the philosophical sort – *Two skeletons are facing each other. One is thinking deeply, chin in hand. "It's very pleasant this life here but I'd really like to know what there is on the other side."*'

'Confounded little idler,' said Mrs. Blue tenderly, 'you are going to fall ill if you go on tiring yourself like this. Well, take this, make the most of your youth…!'

She offered him a 500 franc note.

But he was so lazy she had to slip the note into his pocket herself.

'And now push off,' she said.

* * *

In the music room, furnished with a piano and a bust of Beethoven, René de Fouques was vigorously playing the first chords of a Strauss waltz.

He raised his head and smiled at Agnès.

'You slept well last night, my dear?'

For René de Fouques, lover of Mrs. Blue, was also the lover of Agnès Duffeteaux.

* * *

'Well now, why did you leave your father?' Mrs. Blue gently asked Aimée.

'Well. I left my father because…'

CHAPTER 7

GOUPI – MOUSMÉ

'Aimée was not a rebel. She was happy at home. I always cherished her...'

An autumn rose swayed in front of the window.

Maître Alban Laprade the solicitor was walking backwards and forwards in his office. Mrs. Blue was recalling Aimée's words; this confession which still remained incomplete –

'I left my father because...'

It was not the 'because' of a stubborn child who did not want to reply. Not a refusal, but an inability to explain herself. Like this word 'cemetery' which Aimée was always coming up against – 'My father's house made me think of a cemetery.'

And this solicitor who affirmed – 'Aimée was happy in my home.'

What did he know of happiness and, more to the point, of the happiness of others?

'I refused her nothing, I would not oppose her in anything.'

Awkward in front of this enormous, moustached stranger, he attempted to explain this escapade of his daughter. Or rather, to explain it to himself.

'I refuse to believe that she had listened to bad advice. For a start, I have no enemies.'

He shook his head, conjuring up another possibility.

'An affair, which could have blossomed without my knowing? I refuse to believe it.'

This portly little man, with short, square, thick hands, who did not admit that he could possibly have enemies and who, rolling his r's, 'refused to believe...'

On his desk he had a packet of rough tobacco, cigarette papers all loose, a machine for rolling cigarettes, the simplest model with worn canvas cut away, torn and patched with sticking plaster. There was also a medicine bottle. On the label Mrs. Blue was able to read the prescription number – 3571.

Aimée is a trusting child,' Maître Laprade affirmed. 'Not at all sly or secretive... And I was not just a father to her... I was also a companion. She told me everything.'

'Everything!'

Mrs. Blue stroked her Gengis Khan moustache; it was to conceal a smile behind her extraordinary white hand. As if there existed anyone in the world who told 'everything!'

Furthermore, she reflected, even someone who would have liked to tell everything would not have much to say in this backwater where nothing happened. Where, above the white road, floated only the little dust that would be raised by a cart slowly pulled by two cows. Nor in the inhabitants either was there a possibility of an eruption of first-rate drama: a light swirl of emotions, nosiness, jealousies, quickly dispersed.

A few hundred houses, many unoccupied, dozed in the sun... twelve hundred souls dozing in the drone of tittle-tattle.

Of course, the manageress of St. Agatha's knew that hatred, cupidity, adultery and vice flourished not just in big cities, not by a long chalk. But neither vice, cupidity nor hate were Aimée's thing.

'Boredom?' suggested Mrs. Blue.

'What boredom?' exclaimed the solicitor

Mrs. Blue found the word wonderful.

'We are only twenty kilometres from Angoulême, dear lady. In Angoulême there is a cinema! Repertory companies come. Only recently we played host to the Ladies and

Gentlemen of the Comédie Française. What was it they put on, now?'

He asked through the door.

'Emilie! What did the Artists of the Comedie Française put on recently?'

The Journey of Mr. Perrichon,' Emilie Ranouilh, the secretary, replied from the lobby. She also rolled her 'r's.

'Labiche. Labiche,' he announced triumphantly, 'it's the funniest thing there is.'

'I quite agree,' said Mrs. Blue.

They'd played Labiche at Angoulême! Labiche the tonic! A sovereign cure against boredom! How then could one believe that Aimée had been unable to be happy?

All the same, even *The Journey of Mr Perrichon* had not succeeding in adding to the mind of the young girl enough joyous humour to dissuade her in turn from launching herself on a journey... This hazardous expedition which would have ended God knows where and God knows how, without the providential meeting with Mr. Blue.

'And even so,' Maître Laprade persisted. 'Does one make such an escape through boredom? If Aimée had had the wish to go and spend a few days at the seaside, or in the mountains, or in Paris, to enjoy herself, she would have spoken to me of it! She knew very well that I would not refuse to consider the idea...'

Refuse to consider...

But what had Aimée been able to consider?

'I left my father because I formed the feeling of being in a cemetery ... No, it wasn't because I was idle, nor because everyone seemed dull, gloomy or lifeless ... I left my father because ... .'

Mrs. Blue's glance wandered around the office. The dark green box-files, the heavy works on jurisprudence. But don't all solicitor's offices look the same? With one difference between them, they vary in importance. On this point, Maître Laprade's office was more important than it seemed at first sight...

On getting off the train, Mrs. Blue had sounded out a café owner, a restaurateur, and the postmaster. 'A very, very big practice' they had told her. Behind the shop fronts of the butcher, the haberdasher, the hatter, the man who ran the shoe shop and the cycle shop, there was money aplenty. And the little town represented only a minor part of Maître Laprade's work. There was also the countryside. And in the cupboards of farms there was as much money as in the shopkeeper's wardrobes in the little town! And within a fifteen mile radius all the sales, settlements, loans, life annuities, and all the contracts which were signed passed through Maître Laprade's office. His fortune? Officially, three to four million francs. But it had to be said it was double that!

Six to eight million...

These figures had greatly excited Mrs. Blue.

She scrutinised Maître Laprade, with an eye that she strived to make clinical, and calculated his life expectancy. She would have liked to know what was in the medicine bottle on the desk.

'Aimée's impulse must have affected you very much, my dear sir?'

'You mean that it has almost brought me down! I have a heart condition you see.'

Cardiac... Ah... Interesting that...'

'I've had two attacks already,' he lifted the medicine bottle, 'I take digitalin.'

Two attacks. Never two without three. Mrs. Blue pondered this with satisfaction. 'In any case I'm not destined to make old bones. But with shocks like these...'

This Laprade was really very helpful. There he was now, speaking of his death. It was always fascinating to hear a millionaire saying he will hardly be long before dying. The will must already be written, finalised, in perfect conformity with the rules... After all, he was a solicitor!

In the outer office, which housed the secretary, not a sound... .

When Mrs. Blue had arrived, Emilie Ranouilh was typing unevenly on an old Remington with barely visible type, a hard-wearing model dating from 1900, a model from which occasionally a part fell off. One was not aware what purpose it had served and no-one bothered to replace it. The machine functioned no better and no worse.

'What can I do for you, Madam?'

'I come on a family matter.'

Mrs. Blue knew from Aimée that Emilie was consoling the solicitor in his already long widowerhood. She knew also that there were scarcely any secrets between Alban Laprade and the secretary. But it amused her to make Emilie's tongue hang out.

Since her talk with the solicitor had begun, silence in the outer office. Mrs. Blue pictured the heavy woman, built on the lines of a tobacco jar, holding her breath the better to hear.

'You only have Aimée left, sir,' asked Mrs.Blue.

'She is all that remains to me.'

He pointed out on the wall the photograph of a young brunette with a pale face relegated by huge black eyes.

'The deceased Mrs Laprade.'

'It's amazing how much like her Aimée looks.'

But did she resemble her morally? Had Mrs Laprade, like her daughter, dreamed of running away?

'You see Maître Laprade, let me tell you, speaking as a woman... ("speaking as a woman" – the expression in the mouth of this Hercules in a dress was comical!).

'... boredom in a boy is the wish for adventures, curiosity about far away places, an appetite for action. In short, this takes place in the mind. But boredom in girls is different. It's something organic.'

'Love?' Maître Laprade spoke with disdain. 'But since there has been no love in Aimée's life...'

'Precisely, sir! No love, for a girl, is that living? This little one needs a husband. And children.'

He raised an eyebrow mistrustfully. Whoever talked of

marriage implied a dowry and contract. And he was a solicitor. More than that, a peasant solicitor.

Mrs. Blue knew little of peasants. Enough, however, to make out the age-old depths of shrewdness, calculation and cunning silence transmitted from generation to generation which this man represented.

'A husband,' she repeated, 'children.'

'Perhaps...' He said politely.

'Not "perhaps". Certainly.'

'Yes, undoubtedly', he conceded.

'A son-in-law,' she suggested, who would be able to help you out; take over your practice when you contemplate taking things more easily.'

'Yes, that would be good', he agreed. 'It would be the best thing.' He laughed. 'But all my colleagues have only girls.'

She continued to tempt him.

'In Paris I'm well placed in the world of solicitors and attorneys.' She fluttered her fat, white hands. 'One never knows.' Her hands dropped back gently into her lap. 'Why not?'

'Why not indeed?'

'And if it isn't a solicitor's son or an attorney's,' Mrs. Blue said to herself, 'it will be an English colonel. The important thing is that this girl marries. Ten per cent of eight million, the usual small commission, that makes eight hundred thousand francs'.

The solicitor launched himself into a long tirade to tell Mrs. Blue of his gratitude, the luck that heaven had put her in Aimée's path just at the right moment to prevent the worst.

'As long as she is under your protection, dear lady, I know that she is safe,'

'My boarding house is called the *Protection of the Young Woman*,' Mrs. Blue said suavely, with an episcopal gesture. 'And my brother belongs to the Salvation Army.'

The name of the boarding house, the salvationist brother and, above all, the enormous presence of Mrs. Blue mounting guard in front of the rooms of her "girls", an archangel in petticoats, with the biceps of a champion wrestler. Wasn't this more than enough to discourage the bad lads?

'We're a stone's throw from the Eiffel Tower', Mrs. Blue let drop fatuously – as though the Eiffel Tower added to the notion of safety, to the sense of protection. As if its third platform, touching the heavens, was a designated observation post especially appealing to God.

They reached agreement on several points. Provisionally, Maître Laprade would leave Aimée with Mrs. Blue. He would not write; Mrs. Blue having come to visit him without Aimée's knowledge, it was preferable that the latter remained in ignorance of this arrangement. On the other hand, Mrs. Blue would give the father regular news. She would keep him in touch on the outcome of her lessons and her good advice.

'Aimée goes to Mass,' said Maître Laprade. 'Is there a chapel in your establishment?'

'Alas, no. But I take my girls to St François – Xavier, a stone's throw away.'

A stone's throw. Like the Eiffel Tower! What favourable odds! ... She could even have added 'like the Military Academy!'

The solicitor put a hand on his heart.

Mrs. Blue wondered. The third attack – already?

It was just a surge of emotion. 'You are a saintly woman, madam. God will repay you.'

By association, he enquired about the fees at the boarding house.

'St Agatha's is not a commercial enterprise, my dear sir, but a work of charity. I don't look to make any profit. Let's say ten thousand francs a month?'

She saw that he found the figure rather high.

'Life in Paris is much more expensive than in the

provinces. Three hundred francs a day is a minimum. And if it leaves me with a few hundred francs, that enables me to help indigent girls.'

'That's fair.' He sat down and applied himself, with the attention and respect demanded by such an act, to writing a cheque for the first month.

'A *cemetery*...' Mrs. Blue repeated with amazement. The window to the left, which overlooked the road, revealed to her the touching sight of smocked peasants, using goads on the rumps of cows and sheep in their progress to the cowsheds. The women in head scarves, with geese and chickens in baskets. The window to the right, where the autumn rose was swaying, allowed the sight of a garden in which carnations, asters, marigolds and roses were flourishing. Other gardens were visible in the distance and beyond these extended a plain with poplars, silver in the light. A *cemetery*... where, – the *cemetery* – and why?

Without a doubt because on this plain, in these villages, in this little town, a heart had not been found to beat in harmony with that of Aimée.

'Let us hope that the colonel pleases her,' reflected Miss Blue.

In the outer office the staccato tapping on the Remington had started up again.

Laprade carefully applied blotting paper to the cheque.

'But we had agreed on only ten thousand!' Miss Blue was amazed. The cheque was for twelve thousand francs.

'A mistake, I wasn't thinking.' He dared not take the cheque back to draw up another.

'The supplement will be for your indigents.'

'Thank you on behalf of the dear little ones.'

He wanted her to stay for dinner.

But she knew all she wanted to know.

'My train is in an hour. I'll eat in the dining car. Otherwise I wouldn't be able to get off before tomorrow morning, and I'm anxious not to stay away too long from my girls.'

Saintly woman!

She went to the window.

'You'll allow me to steal from you, my dear sir?'

'Please!'

She picked the autumn rose.

After the saintly woman – the woman!

Eternal Woman! ....

No sooner outside than she went to take a turn into the country. To smoke a cigar. She had been dying for one for two hours.

★ ★ ★

Everyone at St. Agathas was currently being given time off. Mr. Blue was trailing around the Flea Market. The Marthas, only three of them now that Charlotte was in service in the bourgeois apartment in the rue de l'Assomption, were strolling about looking in wonder at the novelties set out by the Jewish stall holders at the Swiss Village not far from the boarding house. Agnès Duffetteaux had gone to see a film, one forbidden to under sixteens; this was the reason which had motivated her choice, and she was hoping it would be really daring! She was comforting herself in thinking of the rendezvous she had made with Réne de Fouques for that evening. Taking advantage of Mrs. Blue's journey, he had promised to take her dancing at a nightclub. Agnès would have liked to get René to marry her. He was elegance incarnate and was enthroned in Montmartre in a studio flat overlooking Paris, which had positively dazzled the girl. And he was a musician! Now, she dreamed of making a career as a musician. But alas, for René to marry Agnès, he had first to break off with Mrs. Blue. How to provoke this split? Agnès pursed her thin lips searching for a shrewd plan. She was dressed a little above the calf; this made her look younger. But in reality she was well past short dresses and her thoughts were long – extensive, gloomy, and tortuous.

On a bench below the Eiffel Tower, Aimée Laprade was chatting with Gérard Blue. He was relating his latest macabre creation:

Two ghosts meet. Both are clothed in old-fashioned winding sheets. 'It's awfully chilly tonight' says one. 'Rather' says the other, 'we can do with a shroud.'

They laughed.

'I've hardly any hope of finding a publisher for my *Joys of the Beyond*. The French, who believe themselves subtle but are simply crafty, don't put up with humour. Even less black humour. Me, I love it!'

With his laid-back style of a great gangling bohemian, eyebrows like a spider's web, hair down to the neck, floppy jacket and clown's trousers, and this charming lack of respect, his habit of fiddling endlessly with shins, thighbones and skull, he seemed to Aimée wonderfully young and alive.

Wasn't that odd? She had left her father's home because she had the feeling there of living in a cemetery and now for a while Gérard, with his airs of a perky Hamlet, had succeeded in persuading her that you can really find amusement only in cemeteries!

With disarming simplicity Gérard spoke.

'Uncle Hippolyte? He's in the Salvation Army like I am a bishop. One day on the bus a salvationist alongside him left her handbag. Uncle Blue returned it to her, he is honesty personified. But he was unable to prevent himself from pinching the Salvation Army card! He doctored it and stuck his photograph on top.'

'What an idea!'

'It amused him. Mr Blue – of the Salvation Army. Just realise how flattering that is! It's like the Lady of the Railway Stations armband. I tell you, he's an innocent. A real child. Those ladybirds, he doesn't just have them on his tie, he has them in his heart, his eyes, his brain.'

And to think that Aimée, in respect of Mr Blue, had had Bluebeard and Landru the notorious serial lady-killers in mind!

She admitted she was having some difficulty getting used to the strange St. Agatha boarding house.

'Of course, it's rather comical as a boarding house. But in fact it's only an employment agency and a marriage bureau, that's all. Beware,' he was laughing, 'my mother is going to try and marry you off. Keep this under your hat. I could get myself into very hot water. I'm putting you in the picture because you look to me like a nice girl. Anyway, you would soon have found out for yourself.'

'You're also nice,' she spoke kindly and added with a smile, 'but in your place I'd still go and have my hair cut.'

He pulled a notebook and pencil hastily from his pocket, to note down a new '*Joys of the Beyond*' which had just sprung into his mind:

'*This one takes place in the catacombs. Thousands of skulls are lined up, one beside the other. A female skeleton comes in, hesitantly. She looks at the skulls and calls shyly "Are you there Edward?"*'

He pulled a face. 'It's not up to much.'

And he went on, 'speaking of nice, someone who is not is René de Fouques.'

'I don't like him either,' said Aimée

This clearly gave Gérard pleasure.

'He was chatting to you earlier on?'

In fact, a little earlier, while Aimée was day-dreaming alone on a bench, René de Fouques had approached her. She could not say that he had been disagreeable; he had spoken to her of concert halls. One afternoon he would take her to one with Mrs. Blue. An hour at a good concert, wouldn't that be worth all the music lessons in the world?

'If Mrs. Blue permits it,' he had continued, 'I will show you my apartment in the rue Ravignan one day. A single room, but very large, on the sixth floor. With a balcony from where I can admire Paris. I have an aquarium of exotic fish and some exotic birds. Sometimes I imagine that the real birds are the fish since their fins, more delicate than feathers, give them the appearance of flying. I also have two dogs, a Skye terrier and a Dandie Dinmont.'

He appreciated only what is refined, luxurious and unusual.

He was more than displeasing to Aimée; he inspired a revulsion in her, something for which, she admitted to herself, she would have been hard put to give reasons. 'I'm definitely not good at explaining things.' But this feeling of revulsion almost bordered on fear.

It had needed the arrival of Blue's son to deliver her from René.

Now, Gérard and Aimée were walking.

'Can I offer you a beer?'

'With pleasure.'

Gérard walked with uncoordinated strides and absurd movements. It made one think of a young dog. Not a pedigree dog – oh no, nothing of a Skye terrier nor of a Dandie Dinmont. A mongrel of the gutter!

He bought roasted peanuts which they nibbled.

Suddenly Aimée, amazed, said 'Mr Hippolyte Blue, your uncle...'

'Yes?'

'He really is your mother's brother?'

'Her brother, yes.'

'Why do they call him Mr Blue?'

'Ah, because that's his name.'

'But then...Your mother's maiden name was...'

'Blue! She was a Miss Blue. And she married a Mr Gaston Blue – my noble progenitor. You'd think that she was devoted to "Blue"! Before setting up St. Agathas she was a teacher in a Catholic school,' he added, changing the subject.

'Your father is dead?'

'No. Gone. A few years ago. He was not a bad man but...
Unreliable...
Transparent...
A ghost.'

He jumped. 'Talking of ghosts... That's it!'

'What!'

My *Joys of the Beyond*. I have it! *We are in the catacombs. There are thousands of skeletons, higgledy-piggledy. A skeleton comes in carrying a pile of shrouds. It speaks. "Don't let me disturb you. It's only the laundry woman!"'*

* * *

Mrs. Blue was drinking white wine at the café in the tiny railway station where those travellers who did not consider the local bus fast enough could, via a local line, connect with the Bordeaux-Paris main line.

A group of farmers was standing around eating and shouting. It was not an argument; it was their usual way of conversing. A habit of talking across fields. Even face to face they shouted at the top of their voices.

Red Hands, who was present, knew them all. To each of them he would have been able to give a nickname. He was asking himself who on earth this moustached woman could be. And Mrs. Blue was asking herself who on earth this wag could be that they called 'Red Hands' or 'The Old Rogue' or 'The Sorcerer'.

The local train came in very slowly, with modesty.

One traveller disembarked. Mrs. Blue got in.

A few moments later a yell rang out in front of the refreshment room.

'Red Hands!'...

'Brother!'...

The traveller and Red Hands slapped each other's backs and moved off arm in arm.

The traveller had come some way, from Marseilles. And even a lot further than that; from Indo-China!

He was twenty-six years of age.

Some of us let ourselves be roused by film posters on which appear scenes of young girls with bursting breasts and inviting thighs. 'Brother' had preferred to yield to the enticements of a poster headed 'French Republic' and decorated with a flag. '*Young Men. Join the Colonial Army.*' He had enlisted for three years, just to see the Empire, to become the young Goupi-Tongking. The three years had become six. And now, he was coming back to the paternal plough! He was returning decorated, wrinkled, weather-beaten, tanned, the whites of his eyes stained with a touch of yellow, eyelid a little slanted, a false Asiatic air, self-important and like a fish out of water. Nevertheless, as a good Charentais, still rolling his 'r's; these he had retained.

'Red Hands! You devilish old villain!'

'Brother! You great idiot!'

As they passed in front of Goupi-Shilling's inn, a tumult of hunting horns burst out – the band were rehearsing *Madeleine* :

Do you know Madeleine?
Madeleine with the long hair ....

Goupi-Shilling was counting money. He had a distinctive way of grabbing coins, as though they were alive and capable of escape; a gesture for catching a grasshopper!

Goupi-Gossip, waiting for the horns to be silent, to allow her to go on chattering, was bouncing Goupi-Lily's youngest child on the counter.

Goupi-Monsieur – a good fellow after all, this Monsieur – was clinking glasses with Goupi-Adage, more idiotic than ever.

'Uncle. What will you have? Goupi-Monsieur asked Red Hands.

'Thanks. I'm with a friend,' said Red Hands.

He took the colonial away to sit in a corner and ordered two Pernods.

'You've got money?' Shilling grumbled. Everyone laughed.

'No. But I'll pay you *in gold*. One of these days.'

An allusion to the treasure! Blackmail. As ever! ...

In the room they were looking at Red Hands with mixed feelings. To some he had done a good turn, as a bone setter. As a sorcerer he had bewitched others, at least so they believed.

'Your good health,' he said to the traveller.

Chance had decreed the meeting. But it was not chance that had encouraged the two men to take a seat on the side.

A third companion had joined them, an invisible person sat facing them, he clinked an invisible glass against theirs. The late Goupi-Tongking, with his big mouth, his manner of the village blusterer and his eye of a mocking bird.

The colonial related his exploits. A few of his exploits. A night was not sufficient had he been obliged to untangle everything.

The final adventure was not the least of them. He was laughing himself.

'Believe it or not, I used to correspond with a Paris chick. Yes, my friend. She was writing to me, I was replying to her... It's silly, but you can't imagine the effect it has on you, to get a letter from a girl when you are out there, in the middle of nowhere, lost in the jungle...'

The jungle! Red Hands recognised Tongking's vocabulary.

'From time to time I sent her a trifle... Oriental slippers, scarf, necklace... That went on for a year. And suddenly, after two years, no more letters. She dropped me! But you'll never guess the best bit. My "Parisienne" – do you know what she was? Indo-Chinese! Yes, my old Red Hands. I had to go over there, to Cambodia, to get into a relationship with a Tongking girl who was living in Paris! Don't you think that takes the biscuit?'

He laboriously extracted a grimy wallet from his jacket pocket and pulled out a dog-eared, creased and greasy photograph.

Red Hands went and planted himself under the light bulb to see better.

'Sweet, eh?'

Red Hands did not answer. His hands were trembling slightly.

'Where was she writing from?'

'I never knew her proper address. I sent my letters to an agency. I didn't put the girl's name on the envelope; I put a number.'

From his wallet Frâlin took out a packet of papers and slipped out an old letter, torn at the folds. He opened it and read :

No. 504, Titmouse Private Post, 57 Boulevard St. Michel, Paris, 5th district.

'A bit like a Poste Restante you could say. She called to collect the letters which came to her number.'

'Why didn't she want you to know where she was living?'

The other shrugged his shoulders.

Red Hands looked at the signature, Humming Bird.

'Humming Bird? What's that mean?'

'It's a name she invented for herself, Miss Humming Bird. I never knew her real name.'

'Like that, you knew neither her name nor address... How did you get to know her?'

'She had put an advertisement in a paper down there – *Young lady of twenty wishes to correspond with serviceman in the Colonial Army*. It's a common thing. It helps to pass the time. And at times it goes further, you know?'

'And you were telling me that it was two years ago...'

'That was it... No reply... nothing! She must have found someone else who knew better than me how to make the pen move.'

At this, 'Tongking' had looked at Red Hands with curiosity.

'Well, well. This photo seems to interest you a great deal?'

Red Hands solemnly showed agreement by nodding his head. Then, after a long silence,

'It's Mousmé! Goupi-Mousmé, my great niece; Goupi-Tongking's daughter. She left me three years ago and I've never had news of her.'

'Well, old chap,' Tongking was dumbfounded, 'no mistake about it, it's a small world!.'

Silence again.

'Colibri. No. 504 Titmouse Private Post, in Paris,' Red Hands repeated. 'That's odd. Would you mind lending me this photo and the letter?'

'You can keep them. Me, I'm finished with women.'

He cast a happy look around him.

'It's good to be back in one's own neck of the woods.'

★ ★ ★

Back in his cabin in the forest, Red Hands lit a candle and made straight for his 'wardrobe', a huge oak chest that he had made himself. He took out a casket and removed from it the letter that Mousmé had left for him on departing three years earlier:

'Red Hands, forgive me. I am fond of you but I am going. I know it is wrong, but I cannot do anything other than leave. I will come back – one day.'

He compared the writing with that on the letter sent by 'Humming Bird' to Tongking.

It was not in the same writing.

He looked again at the photograph.

'But it is Mousmé.'

He closed his eyes to reflect better.

Miss Colibri, No. 504 Titmouse Private Post, Boulevard St. Michel, Paris, No.57, 5th district.

Nodding his head he went to throw a handful of brushwood into the fireplace and slid a match underneath to reheat some beans in which pork rinds were swimmng.

Colibri, No. 504 Titmouse Private Post ...

He went off to draw a bucket of water from Goupi-Dead's well to wash a bowl, a fork and spoon, and a salad of wild dandelion leaves.

Titmouse Private Post, No. 504 …

He looked at the photograph and the two letters.

No. 504, Miss Colibri.

The photo, it *was* Mousmé.

Mousmé and Colibri were one and the same person.

But the letters were in different handwriting.

So it was not Mousmé who wrote the letters signed Colibri.

And yet Colibri was Mousmé.

He went over the conflicting aspects of the problem.

It had begun three years ago. Because three years had passed since Mousmé had left.

But this traffic in correspondence had lasted only a year.

An accident? Mousmé could have injured her right hand, even lost it, and a friend was writing for her.

Come now! If Mousmé had lost a hand she would, all the same, have made it known to Red Hands.

Again, why this brutal silence after one year.

Was Mousmé dead?

★ ★ ★

A week later, as he was removing a large flat stone covering a bucket containing his previous night's catch, a hundred snails, and tipping a fistful of crude salt in to sweat them, he began to grumble.

The same thought was still pestering him…

For a week those words which did not stop going round in his head:

Colibri, 504 Titmouse Private Post

Those two letters which were not in the same hand…

The two names which pointed to the same person…

He returned to the oak chest. From the casket where the

two letters were kept, he withdrew a small stack of thousand franc notes wrapped in newspaper, and counted them, twice over. Next he removed from the great oak chest a dark suit and a large paper bag which contained an extraordinary hard, black felt hat. It was between a top hat in height and a bowler hat by the roundness of the crown. The hat for solemnities – weddings, burial services for the distinguished, and local worthies. In thirty years Red Hands had scarcely worn it more than thirty times. You might as well say it was new.

He took off his cap and put the hat on his head, attempting to ram it down. The hat lifted by itself. His head had widened with time. Even so, it balanced there, provided he moved calmly.

Shrugging his shoulders, he wiped the hat on the back of his sleeve, and carefully replaced it in the paper bag. He tidied away the bag, as well as the suit and casket into the oak chest, and shut the lid. He then went back to sit at the table.

Whilst chewing, he ruminated.

Titmouse Private Post, 504 Boulevard St Michel, No. 57.

What was Mousmé ...

He struck the table with a blow of his fist so violent that his knife, springing from his fingers, spun towards his left hand and gashed the skin in the fold between thumb and forefinger. He did not even notice it.

'I'm going to go see a little of what they look like, those Paris gents.'

Paris – where he had never been... Paris, where peasant crafts are not legal tender and impress no-one. Paris – five hundred kilometres away... In other words, at the end of the world!

It was a tough journey.

But Red Hands really owed this to his nephew Goupi-Tongking. This idiot who, in addition to all the stupid things he had done in his dog's life, had added a worse one; that of producing a daughter.

Red Hands went and emptied the bucket of snails

some metres away from his doorstep. He had decided to leave the following evening. He had no idea how long he would be away. So the snails could get away. Since he would not be eating them, it was pointless to leave them to die.

'Tongking', cross-bred with 'Goupi'.

It was the 'Tongking' which was sending him off on this wild trip.

But it was the 'Goupi' which gave the snails their freedom – nothing must be wasted.

It was only on going back into his hut that he asked himself where the burning was coming from that he felt in the skin fold between his left thumb and index finger.

He went close to the candle.

'Hallo. I've cut the skin.'

There was blood on the hand of Red Hands.

PART TWO

RED HANDS IN PARIS

CHAPTER 8

TITMOUSE PRIVATE POST

Ah well, with his great clogs he had made it here all the same!

'Left at the end of the yard,' the concierge had said.

A shabby door the colour of dried dung. This was it!

TITMOUSE PRIVATE POST.

On leaving Austerlitz station, Red Hands had made an attempt to take the Métro but, almost immediately, had returned to the open air.

'In these cellars I'd quite likely get lost.'

It was not getting lost that frightened him, but of suffocating, he a man of the woods, who could put up with no roof but the sky.

No question of treating himself to a taxi. The Tongking in him had wanted to but the Goupi was strongly opposed! Neither had he taken a bus, having noted that passengers only had right of access on presenting a numbered ticket in response to a call from a conductor wearing a weird cranking mechanism on his stomach. These are subscribers, Red Hands had thought. He had no ticket, and no ticket, no bus.

So he had made his way on foot.

'You only have to go along the Seine as far as Place St. Michel. You can't miss it.'

The woman who had given him the information had watched him for some moments with an amused expression. This fellow both comical and not very reassuring with long hairs in his nose and ears, his deep-set fox's eyes under the peak of his cap, and sharp teeth under a bushy moustache. He was moving off stiffly in his hard-wearing black serge suit cut in the 1900 fashion.

In one hand he carried as a suitcase a wicker basket tied with string. In the other, a large paper bag that he held at arm's length, as though it contained a bomb.

On the kerb he waited at length before dashing onto the Boulevard de l'Hôpital which he crossed in a gallop like a wild boar.

'Pedestrian crossings!' shouted a wag.

Attentive and suspicious, he seemed to have eyes and ears all round his head. A view of the trees in the Jardin des Plantes gave him a surge of emotion. In this infernal city there was at least something human – trees! ...

He had stroked the trunk of a plane tree and then, comforted, began to walk along the river bank. Faced with the thousands of tall houses as far as the eye could see, his first thought had been 'wow, what a lot of stone', and his first feeling, one of being crushed. So, he had preferred to look at the water, still something human...

And now he was contemplating the door of the Titmouse Private Post, that Mousmé must so often have pushed.

He pulled out from the paper bag his extraordinary headgear, half top hat and half bowler hat, put it on his head, and stuffed his cap in the bag in its place.

Then he rang.

Nobody came to open up, although it was eleven in the morning on a working day.

A richly-dressed man coming from the street passed close by, threw him an odd look, and went in. An employee no doubt. 'They don't start their work early here!'

At that moment he noticed above the doorbell a metal plate – ENTER WITHOUT RINGING.

He opened the door so cautiously that he was not noticed.

Standing behind a kind of counter, close to a table where card indexes were laid out, an old maid, looking like a chair attendant from St. Sulpice church, was in discussion with the man who had preceded Red Hands.

'I'm sorry sir,' she was saying, 'but I don't have the right to give you this information! I cannot violate the confidentiality of correspondence.'

'I'm telling you that it's a question of my wife! I'm convinced that she's being written to at your agency.'

'I' can see what it looks like from your point of view, sir. But think about it. If you had letters addressed to yourself here, you wouldn't accept that I show them to other people, right? Above all, to your wife!

'I'm not asking to see them, these letters. I'm only wanting to know whether you are receiving any in her name. Mrs Deshouches. Andrée Deshouches.'

'I don't have the right to know any name, sir. I only know the numbers.'

Along the wall, rows of padlocked metal boxes were indeed carrying numbers.

'It's a matter of professional conscience,' the old woman repeated.

In an angelic voice she insinuated, 'without a professional conscience, think what we could do, sir. Extort money from you, to answer your questions! …. Or extort money from your lady wife for not answering your question! …. In short, blackmail... Horrors!'

The man had a furtive smile, then his right hand, sliding into his half open overcoat, slowly rose to the inside pocket of his jacket... towards his wallet. Without appearing to, the old maid followed the gesture with interest.

Suddenly the sight of Red Hands, lugubrious and solemn under his Derby-type hat, gave her a shock.

'Will you excuse me a moment?' she said to the wealthy man in a near complicitous tone. He took his hand from the inside of his jacket as though it had met a snake.

Red Hands greeted her with a large gesture.

'I've come for Mousmé,' he said.

He put his wicker basket which he had been holding onto down on the counter.

'Mousmé?'

He also put his hat down on the counter but mechanically returned it to balance on his head.

'Goupi-Mousmé, my great niece. She's the daughter of my nephew Goupi-Tongking.'

'Goupi-Mousmé?' The dumb-founded old maid repeated. The wealthy man was watching Red Hands obliquely.

'It's true I'm being stupid,' said Red Hands, 'you won't understand. Mousmé was the nickname she was given, down there in the country. In Paris they call her Humming Bird. That's also nice, Humming Bird.'

He held out over the counter the yellowed and cracked photograph that Frâlin, the ghost from Indochina, had handed over to him.

'Pretty, eh?'

'Very attractive,' said the old maid politely.

'I would like to know her address.'

'We don't give addresses, sir. Our regulation forbids us. And in any case, surely you have made a mistake.'

'Excuse me,' said Red Hands, 'you know how to count up to 504?'

He indicated the rows of padlocked boxes.

'Number 504 – that's hers. That box down there. So don't tell me lies.'

From the conversation of the well-dressed man, he had gathered that nothing was achieved in this Agency with a gentle approach.

'Does she have a time for coming to pick up her post?'

'I'm sorry sir, I can't tell you.'

He slipped a hand into his pocket.

She asked herself whether he could be less of a cretin than she thought.

But in place of bank notes he produced a large knife. She took a step back. He opened the blade and picked his teeth with studied coarseness.

'Listen. I'm called Red Hands and I'm not patient. My niece disappeared three years ago. She got her correspondence sent here, under number 504, from a soldier doing his time in the colonies. All this smells bad and I've decided to get to the bottom of it. I'm not one of those who goes to the police. I work alone. I warn you that if you don't answer me, I'm hopping over your desk and I guarantee that the padlock won't be stopping me from opening Box 504!'

The old maid retreated again and began to shout:

'Miss! … Miss!'

Immediately, a man burst out of the adjacent room. He was a puny specimen with shoulders like a wine bottle. Red Hands could have knocked this absurdity onto his backside just by breathing on him. But it was enough to see his eyes to know that this weed was stuffed with venom. He had the sly look of a crooked detective.

'Mr. Miss,' the old lady spoke, 'I would be obliged if you would intervene. This man,' she indicated Red Hands, 'this man has made threats to me, and…'

'I heard,' replied the person who answered to the name of Mr. Miss. He came over to Red Hands.

'You come from the country, sir. You are not familiar with our ways. You are therefore completely excused. But understand that you have nothing to gain by provoking a fuss. If you are reluctant to address yourself to the police, I am in daily contact with them. A number of these gentlemen honour me with their friendship. This is to tell you,' he followed up by tapping a telephone negligently, 'that if you were not wishing to be reasonable, a call to the police station would be enough for them to send officers of the law here who would calm you down!'

'I assume' said Red Hands, 'that you render small services to "these gentlemen" as you call them?'

Without bothering to reply, the other put a leaflet down in front of Red Hands, underlining a passage. 'Unfailing discretion.'

'Such is our motto and our reason for being. Take this leaflet away, sir. Read it. Think about it. I believe that you will understand that our silence, as distressingly as it may affect you, does us credit. Mum's the word.'

'Excuse me?'

'Mum's the the word – like priests, doctors and lawyers.'

He ran his fingers over a box of card indexes.

'Anyway, I can reassure you without betraying any secret. Box number 504 is reserved for a man. He added comically "word of honour". Consequently, if the young lady your niece honoured us with her subscription under the number 504, it must have been some time ago?'

'Three years, yes,' said Red Hands, 'and the letters stopped two years ago.'

'Well you see then! … . She did not renew her subscription. I hope she is very well and that you find her,' he concluded. 'And if you wish to use our services...'

'I'd be very surprised.'

'Never say "Fountain, I'll never drink your waters again...". To the pleasure of seeing you again, sir.'

'Oh, you'll certainly see me again. You don't know the Goupis,' Red Hands replied, taking up his basket.

He felt a shock. Out in the yard he heard bursts of laughter – laughter of a young lady. For a moment he formed the mad notion that perhaps it was Mousmé! … . It was only a maid, going out with a small child. He slipped the leaflet into his pocket and went off in silence towards the door. There he stopped, turned and caught an ironic expression on the face of the rich man.

'You can smile,' said Red Hands, 'it's my niece I'm anxious about, not my wife. Me, I'm not a cuckold.'

And off he went.

Outside, he put the tight hat back in the paper bag in place of the cap, which he stuck comfortably on his head.

There was a bench opposite the building on Boulevard St. Michel. He sat down and immersed himself in studying the leaflet from the Titmouse Agency.

YOU HAVE AN ADDRESS!

Why not have a POSTAL ADDRESS?

Have you considered that your mail passes through many hands before it arrives in yours? Concierges, servants, employees, family. What a lot of often malicious curiosity! Everyone can examine the postmark, origin, writing and the frequency of your letters, and draw their own conclusions. Avoid your secrets becoming open secrets.

Take a POSTAL ADDRESS outside your home with TITMOUSE PRIVATE POST and you will no longer have to fear indiscretions.

We will receive your post for you under a number or an agreed name. You will benefit in this way from all the advantages that anonymity carries. We will hand over your letters at our counters, or you can collect them yourself in a box reserved for you which you can lock with your personal padlock.

Our watchword and our raison d'être:

UNFAILING DISCRETION!

Passers-by were looking at this fellow with his moustache like a snow-plough who, with his wicker basket and paper bag, was taking up the whole bench.

'What a mess!' Red Hands reflected.

And he translated in blunt terms what the brochure was saying between the lines.

'What are you waiting for, sir, to deceive your wife?... Your mistress will be able to give you a rendezvous with complete safety by writing to you at our offices under a number or an agreed name. And you, Madam, who wish to deceive your husband, need not hesitate. Reserve a box at our Agency that you can lock with your personal padlock! Do not hesitate. Every day that goes by is happiness lost.'

He continued to read:

STAY PUT

You can write or telegraph FROM ANYWHERE AS THOUGH YOU WERE HERE

Our correspondents will be pleased to forward letters and postcards written in your hand. In this way you will avoid social obligations and boring receptions; you will excuse yourself from a missed reception. You will make it appear that you are travelling or away. You will avoid irksome individuals who eat away at your time and independence.

Red Hands went on 'translating':

'Your wife, sir, will believe you are on a business trip in Brittany while you will be in Deauville with your little friend. And you, Madam, will be in Chamonix with your lover while your husband believes you to be in Périgueux, at the bedside of a wealthy old aunt on the point of dying. That is how good marriages are made!

Our watchword and our raison d'être :

THANKS TO THE TITMOUSE AGENCY, CUCKOLDING OCCURS AT ALL SEASONS!

What amused Red Hands above all was the personal padlock. He thought of the chastity belts of earlier times and told himself progress is a fine thing. The padlock, once a guarantee of fidelity, had become synonymous with sleeping around!

Shortly afterwards, he watched all these young people going cheerfully up and down the Boulevard St. Michel. At intervals people went into the building at number 57. Men who were womanising? Women craving sinful liaisons? Two or three times he felt emotional seeing young Indo-Chinese girls go by. Students... Cheerfully they joked with lads. Red Hands was tempted to approach them. 'Would you by any chance know a countrywoman of yours called Colibri?' He dared not. In this environment, where everything was new for him, he had lost his bearings. Only impracticable ideas came to him – poor and feeble ones –

like a tree rooted in arid soil which yields only poor and sickly foliage.

He untied the wicker basket and withdrew a large piece of bread that he had cut from a ten-pound loaf on his departure. He placed a bit of omelette on the top that he balanced with his left thumb. And he gulped huge mouthfuls of bread, covered with only small pieces of omelette. He chewed slowly. From time to time he knocked back a swig of red wine straight from a litre bottle that he then rested on the pavement between his feet. That he might seem ridiculous to passers-by was something to which he was supremely indifferent. He scorned them all as they him, the whole lot of them, these Parisian pigs.

But this bread made from wheat sown and harvested on Charentais earth, and this omelette made from eggs laid by a hen from Charente; this wine produced from grapes gathered from the vines of Charente. All this, which was nothing – but was so much for him! – was saying to him 'What are you up to, coming to Paris? What are you waiting for to get the hell out of here?' He reflected that at this hour, in all the meadows, the young cowherds would be taking home the animals; he thought that the band was rehearsing at Shilling's place; he thought of the snails that he had released last evening, oozing and happy under the bushes.

His head was spinning at seeing all these people around him hurrying, all this hurly-burly of people rushing – rushing after what? Like dust rushes after the wind they did not know, any more than the dust, anything of the wind, the grass, absolutely nothing which is actually reality.

'And it may well be that Mousmé is dead', he told himself. 'And I might stay here for 107 years waiting.'

★ ★ ★

Noon ... one o' clock... two o' clock ... three o' clock.

At rue Ravignon Mrs. Blue was taking tea at her lover's

place. She was smoking strong tobacco in a large pipe. She did not have to stand on ceremony in her lover's home. René de Fouques was sucking a very long amber cigarette holder with a gold band, fitted with a long Pall Mall cigarette. Mrs. Blue was worried. Her thoughts kept returning to the buyers of St. Agatha's and the prediction of her brother that 'Bertrand is going to die'.

And Bertrand was dead!

Maertens .... Berthault .... Gallant .... Roussignac... Bertrand ...

One of them wanted to sell pictures, another luxury dogs, another music and songs, another birds and fish...
Another flowers.

In René's studio the two lapdogs, the Skye terrier and the Dandie-Dinmont, were lying on a rug. There were flowers in vases. On the walls were pretty canvasses, and the exotic fish in an aquarium. There were the exotic birds in the cages. Mellow music flowed from a radio standing on the piano. So, in this room there chanced to be all the components of the terrifying 'curse' which had shrouded the humble St. Agatha boarding house, like a blood-tinged cloud, for so many months.

As for these crimes, if that is what they were, one single conceivable motive – to prevent the selling up of the business. Put another way, to oppose the departure of Mrs. Blue and her brother. But in what way was the presence of Mrs. Blue and Hippolyte Blue at Avenue Floquet able to...

Did they unknowingly facilitate who knows what secret traffic, that other tenants of the building, by virtue of their arrival, would have made impracticable?

The explanation was even more grotesque than the enigma.

St. Agatha's was earlier called The Wasp Waist. Bras, corsets, girdles, suspender belts, garters, lingerie. The shop was run by the Cérisolles. More precisely by Mrs. Louise Cérisolles, who saw the customers, carried out the fittings and made the alterations. Jean Cérisolles busied himself with the accounts, taxes, stocking up and deliveries. The husband was a sad, silent man with a long face. His wife was a small redhead; no great beauty but vivacious. He was from the East, she from the south of France. She had the Avignon sun in her blood ; he had the rain, the slow, everlasting, silent and sad rains of Lorraine. Then one day the cardinal points had split up! That is, Mrs. Cérisolles had fled with a boyfriend. The long, sad face of the abandoned husband was then left in this setting of fripperies! This cuckold, touching with his long, sad fingers the frivolities, the symbols of intrigue, the accessories of seduction, the pepper and the spices of feeling...

He had tried to hold on, employing an assistant. Without being a flourishing business it was, after all, manageable without the unfaithful redhead. But it was Jean Cérisolles who was unable to manage without her; he was unable to continue breathing in this shop where everything reminded him of his misfortune. He could not continue to sell these same weapons of sexual arousal which had helped Louise to elope. He could not continue to receive customers. They were coquettes for the most part who came there with adulterous ideas, looking for supplementary assets to their attractions.

He had sold the lease to Mrs. Blue.

Between the hopeless Cérisolles and the five-fold matter of Maertens, Berthault, Gallant, Roussignac and Bertrand, no connection was conceivable.

So... ?

In her mind's eye Mrs. Blue ran over the premises of St. Agathas, top to bottom. Low ceilings, very compartmentalised, poorly ventilated and meanly lit.

By a natural progression this line of thought brought up another question mark. What a ludicrous notion on the part of these five to have made them set their hearts on this long string of narrow rooms, bathed in gloom; on these musty rooms for faded dolls. In order to set up businesses all calling very much for spacious, airy, well-ventilated and bright places – a picture gallery, a flower shop, aquaria, dog kennels, birdcages, and those other 'birdcages' where lovesongs dear to the public's heart billed and cooed; music boxes!

Clearly, with ten small rooms one can make one large one. With two floors and low ceilings one could have a workshop. But at what cost!

On the other hand, the rent was minimal, the cost of transferring the lease very low, and the area so chic.

Mrs. Blue made an imperious gesture. René de Fouques immediately turned the knob on the radio. Silence. One could have said that even the exotic birds from the islands had stopped their chirruping in Japanese or Maori; the dozing lapdogs stopped growling in their dreams, and the magnificent Pacific fish seemed to become even quieter than fish – all to allow Mrs. Blue to reflect.

'Little mouse,' she said. It was the pet name she gave her lover, 'little mouse, I believe I've had a brilliant idea.'

'That doesn't surprise me, big one,' replied René.

She poured herself a glass of cognac.

Between Maertens, Berthault, Gallant, Roussignac, and Bertrand she had suddenly established a common factor – all of them wanted to set up a business of luxury goods.

Perhaps that was the key?

Stretched out on a divan, in the forbidding but protective shadow cast by the full armour of Gonzague de Fouques, a fifteenth century ancestor, René was watching Mrs. Blue meditating.

But she made a gesture of discouragement. The 'luxury' idea was leading nowhere.

She emptied her glass of cognac, tapped the bowl of her pipe against an ashtray, left her white hands to flutter for a moment, and stood up.

'Little mouse, I must leave you. I must go and find my girls.'

As soon as she had gone, René ran to the very end of

the apartment to release Aimée Laprade, locked in a lumber room converted into a wardrobe. After lunch, on the pretext of going to rummage in the boxes of the booksellers on the embankment, on the lookout for the works of English poets in the original, Aimée had left St. Agatha's to come to René de Fouques apartment. As for Mrs. Blue, she had left the boarding house intending to visit this English colonel, whom it would not have displeased her to betroth for an honest commission to Aimée, or Agnès, depending on the colonel's choice. She had missed the colonel who was in some club.

'What if I popped round to my lover's place?'

So that Aimée had barely had time to take a fearful look at the wonders of the studio of rue Ravignan when Mrs. Blue, dropping by unexpectedly, had pressed René's bell with the usual three, brief rings. René just had time to hide Aimée.

'Three rings, it's a colleague of mine. A friend of Mrs. Blue. A delightful lad but a gossip. Better he doesn't know that you're here.'

Why, in preference to a stroll in the company of the bizarre Gerard Blue, for whom she nevertheless felt a real empathy, had Aimée accepted this meeting with René de Fouques, despite the irritation and near revulsion that he produced in her?

But perhaps it was just because of this irritation and near revulsion?

This person, to the extent that he was still disturbing, brought out she wouldn't say what fascination.

'Could it be that I'm only a tart? She asked herself naively while he poured her tea, offering her some petit fours.

After a short chat, during which René showed himself the perfect gentleman, permitting himself neither a risqué gesture nor word, Aimée took herself off to return to St. Agatha's. René had lent her a Tennyson and a Shelley. She would say that she had found them in the bookshops.

★ ★ ★

Three-thirty ... Four o'clock ... Four-thirty.... On the Boulevard St. Michel, Red Hands was continuing with his guard duty.

From time to time, the concierge at number 57 cast an intrigued glance at the stubborn peasant who smoked pipe after pipe.

A little before five o'clock, a man of about sixty, dressed in a purple corduroy suit, went into the building. He had a long, thin beard. Through the fan of scanty hair the pattern of his tie was visible – blue and red ladybirds.

Ten minutes later he reappeared carrying half a dozen small packets of various shapes tied together with scruffy string. The string broke and the packets fell. The wrapping around one of them, already torn, burst.

The man grumbled and put all his parcels on the road side of the bench, that is, opposite to that cluttered with Red Hand's basket and hat. He retied his string, then pulled on it – but the string was no good so the parcel broke open again.

Red Hands dipped a hand into his jacket pocket where he kept a length of sheaf-binding string, always useful. He prepared to offer it to the bearded man whom he saw sideways by turning his head slightly. But the latter, giving up the idea of tying his parcels up, had decided to stuff them into his pockets. He unwrapped the torn paper. Seeing the object that the paper had contained put Red Hands off offering his string.

It was an ugly ivory statuette in the Chinese style.

Chinese – Indo-Chinese... Red Hands lacked even the simplest notion of artistic culture. But often, in Goupi-Tongking's 'straw hut' he had seen horrors like this, brought back from the colonies by his fool of a nephew.

The man with the scanty beard threw into the gutter the paper which had wrapped the statuette and took himself off.

Red Hands quickly skirted round the bench and grabbed the wrapping paper. He was startled when he read the address. Everything in Paris undoubtedly went on at full gallop, even luck, even chance:

>Number 504
>Titmouse Private Post
>57 Bd. St. Michel
>Paris. Fifth District
>FRANCE

Mr. Miss had not lied. The subscriber of number 504 was a man. The sender also was a man, a sergeant stationed in Siam. The postmark showed that it had been posted in Bangkok. And the stamps were Indo-Chinese. They showed a junk, except one, which depicted a young and attractive Indo-Chinese girl with a solemn expression.

This examination had only taken a few seconds. Red Hands removed from the paper a rectangle bearing the sender's address, that of the addressee, the postmarks and the stamps. He slipped it into his waistcoat pocket, took the bag containing his hat, the wicker basket, and rushed off in pursuit of the man with the parcels.

Along the rue de l'Ecole-de-Médecine, the one following on from the other, they reached the Boulevard St. Germain. On the way, the sign on a café intrigued Red Hands, Les deux Magots (actually the two monkeys, but also means the two hoards of money!) He thought of the Goupis. They had just one hoard of money and that was enough to drive them mad!

They went on... Because of the traffic, crossing streets gave the countryman cold sweats. Fortunately, on the bench in the Boulevard St. Michel, the bearded man had paid no attention to Red Hands. Thus, he had no reason to suspect this peasant who was trailing around a wicker basket. This simplified the shadowing.

The man turned into a narrow sreet – the rue Du Dragon. He went into No.14. Shortly after he came out again; his pockets were empty but now he carried a bag of waterproof cloth.

At Place St. Germain-des-Prés he took the Métro. In these underground corridors Red Hands suffered again the feeling of suffocation. A stupid incident almost put a premature end to his trailing – the few minutes he had to lose at the ticket office buying a ticket because, not knowing the outcome of this chase, he asked for a ticket for 'going as far as the end.'

'What end?' the official wondered

'Well. That's where you can't go any further. Me, how do I know? I'm not from Paris.'

'There is no end,' the official was smiling, 'it goes round you see? By changing at the connections you can travel all day, if that amuses you.'

He then enquired, more obligingly 'where are you going?'

'I'd very much like to know!' retorted Red Hands, and ran off.

Luck continued to favour him. He caught up with the bearded man grumbling at a barrier which had been shut in his face.

They changed at Châtelet and took the line to Porte de Clignancourt.

Ten minutes walking took them to an incongruous place – the Flea Market. The abundance and diversity of objects on display on the rows of stalls astonished Red Hands. He wanted to stop everywhere, so much was interesting. But the bearded man, who appeared to be at home here, was threading his way cheerfully in this maze of galleries. In passing, he gave a brief acknowledgement here and there to a stall owner.

Eventually he stopped in front of a stall.

'Hallo there, Mr. Blue. What have you brought me that's good today?' The trader enquired.

'The exotic as usual,' said the visitor. 'Exotica! More

exotica! Always the exotic – and France will be saved.'

He pulled from his bag a number of objects of Asian or African provenance. A scarf, two kimonos, a crocodile leather bag, a negro statuette, the vaguely Chinese statuette mentioned earlier, three orange amber necklaces, sculpted ivory, bracelets, a strange musical box encrusted with mother-of-pearl, and even a twist of elephant hair. The collection was evaluated in the blink of an eye, the passing of seven thousand-franc notes from the stallholder's wallet to Mr. Blue's, a handshake, and a 'till next time'.

And Mr Blue went off again with Red Hands on his heels. These Parisians transact really fast. In Goupi territory it would have been a full day of discussions!

The Métro again, to Porte d'Orléans. Change at Strasbourg St. Denis. Direction Balard. Mr. Blue got off at La Motte-Picquet. Shortly after, he arrived at Avenue Charles Floquet. Gérard Blue was coming towards him with his gangly walk and he quickly hid the bag under his jacket.

'Hey, Uncle Hippolyte! Would you believe I"ve just found a fantastic story for my Joys from the Beyond. In the chest cavity of a skeleton between the ribs in the heart area a chaffinch, as in a cage. The bird is singing. The skeleton says to another "I don't know what's going on with me but I feel a joyful heart." '

'That's sweet.' Mr. Blue was appreciative.

He went on, guffawing, into a single-storey house over the door of which one read:

ST. AGATHA INSTITUTION
Protection of the Young Woman

Red Hands did not hesitate. He went to buy a candle from a nearby tobacconist, then returned towards St. Agatha's. On the doorstep he put on his half-bowler, half-opera hat and stuffed his cap and the paper bag into his jacket.

And he went in.

CHAPTER 9

'MR' RED HANDS

'I'm sorry Mr. Goupi. Miss Colibri was actually at St. Agatha's for a year. But it was two years ago that she left me, without a reason and without an explanation. Since then, nothing! I don't hold it against her. You can't hold it against young people. But all the same …'

'Yes of course, Mrs. Blue.'

'She went out one morning, supposedly to buy lipstick, and didn't come back. I looked for her suitcase but didn't find it. She must have left it in a café the day before. I alerted the police and they searched, with no result. Ah! You wouldn't have seen such things in the old days Mr. Goupi.'

'Call me Red Hands. The Goupis are the others – my family...'

Me, of course, I am another breed! Like Tongking, Colibri's father!' He laughed.

Mrs. Blue laughed. And the three apprentices of Mrs. Blue, the three farm girls destined for service in middle-class establishments, were laughing.

As it is they had already laughed at the entry of this moustachoed fellow into the 'classroom', wicker bag in one hand, formal opera hat in the other.

Mrs. Blue and Red Hands soon recollected their meeting in the refreshment room of the little country station.

'You have come to see Aimée Laprade?'

He had almost cried out 'What! Aimée Laprade here?' But suspicious by nature, he had held his tongue.

'Excuse me, Madam. I'm coming for Mousmé, my great niece.'

'Mousmé?'

'Colibri, if you prefer.'

'Ah, Colibri! ....An Indo-Chinese?'

'That's it.'

At that moment Mr. Blue had come in. He did not react to the sight of Red Hands, so he had not registered that the latter had shadowed him.

Red Hands was glad not to have mentioned that he was unaware of Aimée Laprade's being at the boarding house and further, not to have spoken of 'Brother' and of the letter signed by Colibri.

Indeed, he wondered now whether it was not simply the bearded man himself who was writing the love letters...

These letters did not give St. Agatha's address. So that Red Hands could not claim that it was 'Brother' who had told him of the boarding house in Avenue Floquet without the risk of alerting the bearded man.

'It was Maître Laprade who advised me to come and see you,' he said blandly. 'Last week, I spoke to him about Mousmé. "Perhaps she did the same as my daughter" he told me. "Perhaps she is at St. Agatha's?"'

He let the words out only with care. Peasants have the reputation of speaking slowly and he played on it. It was not so much the bearded man who impressed him, as Mrs. Blue. He guessed he was dealing with a formidable creature, with whom he had to watch his step. This old biddy was a super-Goupi type. Also, two things worried him.

First, what sort of boarding house was St. Agatha's, for heaven's sake? Second, that Miss Laprade had come here to advance her studies, that was quite normal. But Mousmé? Mousmé, who had never got further than elementary school... Mousmé, who did not have a penny.

'I take in young girls who have run away from their

homes.' Mrs. Blue said. 'I prevent them from misbehaving.' She corrected this. 'At least, I try!'

'There you are!' said Red Hands.

The three young girls regarded him furtively. This countryman who rolled his r's, it was as if with him there, their native soil had come to pay them a visit in the big city. And to a certain extent, just by being there, these buxom flowers of the field helped to keep the somewhat unseated Red Hands in the saddle.

'I'm rather at a loss,' he said 'if the police weren't been able to find Colibri in two years, I shan't manage it!'

'I'm sorry Mr. Red Hands. If you had written to me I could have saved you the journey,' implied Mrs. Blue.

'You know, I'm not a great writer.' He did his best to act the idiot.

Mrs. Blue smiled.

'And besides,' Red Hands concluded, 'I've never been out of Charentes. It was an opportunity to see Paris.'

'In fact, you're going to visit it, I hope?'

'Since I'm here. I'm staying three or four days.'

'Miss Laprade will be able to make you take some walks. She's not a notable Parisienne yet but already she is managing very well. She will show you the main monuments. The Arc de Triomphe, the Eiffel Tower which is two steps away, Notre Dame, the Opéra. You can't leave without having been to the Opéra, Mr. Red Hands!'

If it upset Red Hands to be called 'Mr. Goupi', it was frankly comic to hear 'Mr. Red Hands' being used.

Mrs. Blue sent for Aimée.

'By the way,' she confided to Red Hands, 'I would be grateful to you for not telling her that Maître Laprade gave you my address, nor that I went to his place. She doesn't know that I have told her father she is with me.'

'Understood.' Red Hands said.

He ran his eyes over the Louis XV armchairs, the

ornamental patterns of the Jouy cretonne print, the erotic little paintings.

'It's a pretty classroom! A great deal more cheerful than the primary school in our place!'

'Indeed! We are in Paris', said Mrs. Blue, with a stylish flight of her wonderful chubby, white hands.

Aimée pushed open the door, trembling. She thought of finding her father but at the sight of the Goupi she relaxed a little.

'Red Hands!'

But she bristled immediately. 'My father sent you?'

'Well, no. And you are certainly the last person I was expecting to meet here, Miss Aimée. I came up to Paris to see my niece, Tongking's daughter, you remember?'...

'Mousmé? Of course,' said Aimée. 'But I didn't know she had been to St. Agatha's.'

She smiled, reassured.

Gérard came in and Mrs. Blue made the introductions.

'I believe we are almost colleagues?' Red Hands spoke.

The young man was dumbfounded.

'I'm a gravedigger in my little village,' explained Red Hands. 'Earlier, in the street, I heard you talking of the cemetery. You are in the funeral business?'

Amused, Gérard put the record straight.

'In actual fact,' he concluded humorously, 'since you dig graves, you might possibly give me some ideas for my skeleton tales.'

As Red Hands took his leave, he asked whether someone could not recommend him a hotel.

'Something reasonable. I hate being stung.'

Mr. Blue suggested the Hôtel de l'Espérance, rue du Laos.

'You could note the address on this for me,' Red Hands offered a pencil with the paper that was used to wrap his hat.

While Mr. Blue was writing, Red Hands took from his pocket a box of sulphur matches and the candle bought at the tobacconist opposite.

'I'm taking precautions. I'm armed.'

'Armed?'

'To light up during the night.'

'But there is electricity!'

'I can well believe it. Except, I have done without it all my life and...'

'You're wrong. It's very convenient. You press on a switch and...'

' ... And burn yourself!' Red Hands replied.

He took the paper bag upon which Mr. Blue had written the address and carefully placed his hat inside it. Taking out his cap, he put it on with quiet good-heartedness and took his leave.

He had not gone fifty metres when he heard Aimée running behind him.

'Mrs. Blue has given me permission to take you to rue du Laos.'

Then, after a silence, 'Tell me Red Hands... If you were kind...'

He finished for her. 'I would not tell Maître Laprade that you have landed up at St. Agatha's?'

She nodded. They went a few more steps, Aimée, still without looking at Red Hands :

'You must be asking yourself why I have...'

'Why you ran away from your father's home? It's not a habit of mine to ask questions about things which aren't my business.'

'I don't know very well myself why I ran away,' she admitted.

'But me, I know why,' he spoke softly. 'It's because you are a "Tongking". They can't avoid doing stupid things.'

'A "Tongking?" ... I don't follow.'

'Me, I know what I mean. Anyway, don't worry. I'll not say anything.'

They were approaching rue du Laos.

'On reflection,' said Red Hands, 'I won't put up at

l'Espérance. On our way, I noticed an hôtel nearby called the Hôtel des Charentes.'

Then, out of the blue.

'What sort of people are your Mrs. Blue and her brother?'

'Good souls. A bit odd, especially the son, with his skeleton stories. And Mr. Blue with his craze for taking photographs.'

'Oh yes?' said Red Hands sharply. 'What does he photograph?'

'Well, everything... All the young ladies at St. Agatha's. He photographed me from the day after I arrived. Full face, profile, three-quarter view. He even photographed me with a fur coat of Mrs. Blue's over my shoulders. He dreams of setting up an art studio.'

'That's interesting,' said Red Hands in an odd voice which Aimée did not notice.

'They are very kind, very charitable,' she continued. 'They make no money with St. Agatha's. It's a philanthropic organisation.'

'All the same they don't live on air?'

'I suppose they get a small subsidy from the council.'

In rue Tiphaine, a narrow street parallel to the Boulevard de Grenelle, Red Hands stopped in front of a hôtel of more than modest appearance.

'This is it. If ever you have something urgent to tell me, you will know where to find me.'

They shook hands.

'In Paris, Mousmé had called herself Colibri,' Red Hands said again. 'Did anyone speak to you about her at St. Agatha's?'

'No. No-one. I can ask Gérard Blue.'

'That would be very kind of you. Do it discreetly. Perhaps they know where she is but she doesn't want me to be informed – like you with your father?'

The Charentes hôtel was full of North African immigrants.

'You are Charentais? Red Hands asked.

The manager was from the Auvergne.

'Pity, because I'm Charentais. You have many Charentais as customers at the moment?'

With a limp gesture, the manager pointed out the group of immigrants.

'My customers are from Oran, Bône, Algiers.'

'Ah,' Red Hands was disappointed, 'from your sign I would have hoped...'

'That's to say the man who kept the hôtel before me was himself from Charentes.'

'He went back to the country?'

'No. He died.'

'Go on. That's too bad.'

A porter accompanied him to his room on the ground floor. While the porter closed the shutters, Red Hands emptied his pockets onto the mantelpiece – knife, tobacco and pipe, string, candle. The porter pressed a light switch near the door.

'There's another switch over your bed. Do you need anything, sir?'

'If you could bring me a litre of red wine. House wine.'

The porter returned with a bottle and a glass, together with a traveller's form to fill in. Red Hands had opened the case of his watch, a very old one which was wound up with a key.

'Shall you want waking in the morning, sir?'

'No need. I get up with the sun.'

'The toilets are at the end of the corridor. Good night, sir.'

★ ★ ★

At St. Agatha's Mrs. Blue was closeted with her brother. She was extremely agitated.

'I don't like this visit at all! Let's hope that this Red Hands doesn't bring us problems.'

'What problems?'

'Suppose he goes to the police and sets off an enquiry about Colibri.'

So what? She disappeared, we aren't involved...'

'Any more than we are involved in the business of Maertens, Gallant, Roussignac, Berthault and Bertrand. Nevertheless it begins to add up.'

Hippolyte Blue shrugged his shoulders.

'First of all, this fellow is not the type who gets involved with the police. He's going quietly back to his village.'

He burst out laughing. 'I never would have believed that there could be people so behind the times. You saw the joke with the candle? He's frightened of burning himself putting the lights on.!'

★ ★ ★

In his room, under the light bulb, Red Hands was examining carefully the address of the Hotel de l'Espérance written on the paper bag by Mr. Blue. He compared the writing with that on the letter signed 'Colibri'. He noted that what he suspected was true – the author of the Colibri letters was Mr. Blue. It was precisely to verify this that Red Hands had requested Mr. Blue to write down the hotel address.

He sat on the bed, eating the remains of his bread and omelette eased down with red wine, and began to reflect.

'Mr. Blue takes photographs of the young ladies who come to end up at his sister's home. He puts advertisements in colonial papers, seeking to correspond with soldiers, to whom he sends photographs of the young ladies accompanied by sentimental letters written by himself. The soldiers reply to him and send presents which he sells at the Flea Market. Of course, the young ladies are unaware of any of these intrigues.'

What precisely this trickery meant, and whether it was related to the disappearance of Mousmé, Red Hands sought in vain to work out. But one point seemed to him to have been established.

Mr. Blue subscribed to the Titmouse Private Post so that his sister, on whom he sponged, was unaware of his fine dealings.

Red Hands calculated that this gave him a promising trump card over friend Hippolyte.

He knocked back another swig of red wine and decided to sleep.

He looked at his candle on the mantelpiece and smiled. Then, without fear of burning himself, put on the light over his bed, went over to the switch near the door to put out the main light, lay down, switched off the bedside light and closed his eyes.

In the small hours he was awakened with a start by a thought. Not important but it confirmed what he had already discovered.

Why had 'Brother' suddenly stopped receiving letters signed by Colibri? Simply because the gifts that the good fellow was sending, slippers, scarf, knick-knacks, were not sufficiently marketable. Mr. Blue had calculated that that game was not worth the candle.

Without switching on the light he got up. He did not go to the trouble of visiting the lavatory at the end of the corridor. What was the point since his room was on the ground floor? He opened the window, pulled the shutters slightly aside and emptied his bladder into the street. Just as he did every night in his hut in the forest in Goupi territory.

He had no intention of putting himself out and changing his habits on the pretext that he had come to pay a visit to these Parisian gentlemen!

CHAPTER 10

THE SECRET OF ST. AGATHA'S

He had said, 'I'll stay three or four days and take myself off...'

But he had now been there a good week.

Every evening he repeated, 'All the same, I must take the road to Austerlitz station.'

But the following morning they saw him going into the boarding house, contented and full of fun, his cap on his head, his half-bowler, half-opera hat in the paper bag. He was becoming a regular visitor. He had long chats with the Marthas on farming, what was chiefly harvested in their region, whether they worked with cows or horses, and so on...

It amused Hippoyte and particularly Gérard, for whom Red Hands had even dredged up a rather saucy skeleton story that the young man had adopted for his collection:

There are two skeletons in shrouds, male and female. The male is seated on a grave, the female standing nearby. Her shroud is blown out in the front. 'Ah-ha! .... An interesting condition?' Says the male. 'No, come on now,' explains the female, 'it's the wind.'

They had him stay to lunch and after the meal obligingly listed the monuments of Paris that 'Mr. Red Hands' had to visit.

'What interests me are the cemeteries', he said.

He left with Aimée, ostensibly for the noble Père-Lachaise, or the delightful Passys cemetery, or the dog's cemetery, so comical and touching. But they didn't go further than the Eiffel Tower, the sight of which plunged Red Hands each time into dismay. He could not comprehend anything more grotesquely useless than this vain pile of scrap iron, this apalling Meccano set for giants. They sat on a bench; he lit his pipe, casting a sad eye over Champs-de-Mars. All this arable land, where one could have beets or corn coming on.

'Has Gérard told you anything interesting about Colibri?'

Sadly, Gérard's revelations were limited to very little. At St. Agatha's, Colibri had said nothing of her past. She was very secretive, like most Eastern girls. They resemble one another and all have the same mysterious nature. Colibri fixed her big dark eyes on you and gave the impression of reading you. As for reading her, that was another kettle of fish.

'Yes, that's right. That's absolutely right,' said Red Hands.

'She was gentle and sweet. She seemed neither happy nor unhappy.'

'Yes, yes, absolutely right.'

'So that no-one understood anything about her departure, about which she had not confided to anyone.'

'That's absolutely it! ... But I'm no further forward than before!'

He directed the conversation towards Mr. Blue. Aimée told Red Hands of her meeting with "The Lady of the Railway Stations" at St. Lazare.

'That's certainly how he made the acquaintance of Colibri – at Austerlitz station,' Red Hands agreed. 'He loves doing good, that man.'

He knew now that this impressive Mr. Blue had never belonged to the Salvation Army, despite the FORWARD magazine that one always saw sticking out of his pocket.

And his Salvation Army card. "A fake, stolen identity. Enough to land him in court!" Red Hands said to himself with satisfaction.

'And Gérard, what do you think of him? He seems a

good fellow. And he could have a fondness for you; that wouldn't surprise me.'

Aimée agreed with a smile.

Red Hands did not enquire whether Aimée's feelings responded to Gérard's. It was enough to look at the girl, her pink cheeks, her lowered eyelids. He smiled to himself at the face that Maître Laprade would make if ever he saw this young man turning up in his office to ask for Aimée's hand.

'Shall we go to Père-Lachaise?' she suggested eventually.

'Well, no! I prefer going back to Les Halles, or La Villette. Tombs, they interest me well enough, but vegetables or livestock, they interest me even more!'

They agreed on a time and a place to meet up, near St. Agatha's, and parted company – he supposedly going to see cabbages and carrots, calves and sheep; she to go and meet up again with...

She did not say with whom, but Red Hands guessed only too well. She had a fondness for Gérard Blue and a revulsion for René de Fouques.

But she was going to René's!

This revulsion was a bizarre mixture of fear and curiosity.

The dubious side of the musician held an attraction for her of which she was ashamed – deliciously.

She went into a café to telephone René and find out whether she could visit.

'My God, I'm so complicated,' she said to herself as she dialled, 'I must be bad at heart.'

'But of course,' said René at the end of the line, 'come quickly, I'm waiting for you.'

She took the Métro, the poor girl analysing herself. She built up a whole literature on her case. 'It must be something in the nature of fascination, or bewitchment. I'm overcome by vertigo.' She repeated the word – vertigo, vertigo – deliciously.

Memories of religious reading came back to her. *Lucifer was the most beautiful of the angels ...* Memories of retreat ... *The greatest trap of the devil, my children, is his beauty ...* She reflected on sin. Going like this, clandestinely, to the studio in rue Ravignan, surely this was a sin. She was wildly excited by this thought – 'I'm playing with fire. I'll end up damning myself...'

Rue Ravignan, and another temptation from the devil – vanity. She recalled the fable of the struggle of Mr. Seguin's goat with the wolf. She too would struggle. She felt strong, so strong. She went up the stairs shivering – again deliciously.

Red Hands had seen René de Fouques only once, at the boarding house. The musician had given Gérard Blue a skeleton story (these stories were steadily becoming a mania at St. Agatha's; everyone set about concocting them, even the Marthas).

Needless to say, that of René's touched on music:

Before a seated audience of skeletons, an orchestra of skeletons was striking up 'Danse Macabre.' Immediately, all the skeletons stood to attention save one, probably day-dreaming. A skeleton touches him on the shoulder. 'stand up, old chap. The National Anthem.'

Red Hands had disliked René de Fouques from the outset and he could not see him without feeling in his palms a wish to box his ears.

While Aimée was drinking tea at rue Ravignan, Red Hands was watching out for Mr. Blue near the Titmouse Agency.

In the evening he met up again with Aimée near St. Agatha's. He bought a large rib of steak at the nearest butcher. They returned as accomplices to the "Protection of the Young Woman".

'I've dragged this poor young lady again to La Villette,' he announced to Mrs. Blue, 'it reminds me of back home.'

He proudly took out his steak. 'A friend gave me this.'

Naturally Miss Blue invited him to dinner.

'You're incorrigible Mr. Red Hands. Your country isn't going to disappear, for God's sake. You'll see it again. Whereas Paris...'

One evening she decided, 'I'm taking you along to a show!'

She took him to the Folies Bergère. He saluted the bemused usherettes with large gestures of his ceremonial opera hat which he refused to leave in the cloakroom. He kept it on his lap.

On the stage a chorus of girls, the most beautiful in the world the programme assured him, raised their legs conscientiously without arousing him.

'Like those girls,' sighed Mrs. Blue comically during the interval, 'I also had exciting thighs around thirty. Nowadays obviously the matter no longer arises. I have my loves like everyone else, but I know the price they cost me.'

She offered Red Hands a toffee. They smiled.

But this ample woman's smile hid inadequately the vague dread which was beginning to come over her with the stubborn presence of this poacher come up from the back of beyond to look for his Indo-Chinese great niece. This thickset fellow with a veiled look, slow speech, slow hands, awkward gestures. This man with the small eyes of an elephant...With the patience of an elephant...

And Red Hands, coldly watching the girls rhythmically lifting their exciting thighs, repeated to himself 'You, my good Mrs. Blue, you know what's become of Mousmé. I'll stake my all on it. And I'll bet my bottom dollar that I'll find out, or I'll lose my name of Red Hands!"

★ ★ ★

That evening in the Marys' dormitory Agnès questioned Aimée craftily in her shrill voice about René de Fouques.

Aimée maintained a prudent reserve.

'If you promise not to tell,' Agnès murmured, leaning towards her companion's bed, 'I'll tell you something extraordinary.'

Aimée promised.

'René de Fouques sleeps with Mrs. Blue. Don't you think that's dreadful?'

'Dreadful.'

She imagined René in the arms of Mrs. Blue and felt herself blushing to the roots of her hair.

René had made a date with Aimée for the following evening.

She would not go. She would never go again, absolutely not!

She would have repeated this to herself even more emphatically, had she suspected that her companion knew her secret.

That afternoon, the venomous Agnès, jilted by René, and with her talent for sniffing out intrigues, had followed and spied on Aimée.

She had seen her go into the apartment building in the rue Ravignan!

Beside herself with jealousy, she had seen Aimée's figure close to René's, outlined up there in the sky on the balcony of this studio more beautiful than Paradise.

★ ★ ★

During the night Aimée was awakened by muffled bangs. They came to her in the confusion of semi-sleep when places are recalled with only a vague consciousness; the girl believed she was in her father's house. She fell asleep again and these muted sounds produced a dream of woodcutters felling trees in the pine woods of Charente.

Now, down in the cellar of St. Agatha's, Mrs. Blue, in her night clothes, was digging.

She heard a step on the stairs. She felt that her heart

had stopped beating, and all of a piece she swung round.

Mr. Blue, in his purple dressing-gown, was coming down the spiral staircase.

'Well done, little sister. I see you've had the same idea as myself.'

He came close to the hollow she was digging and pulled an admiring face.

'You have hit the bullseye first time! Me, I began wasting time poking around in the walls...'

In the hollow was a skeleton!

He bent over and picked up the skull.

'I don't know whether Gérard, being crazy about skeleton stories, would like this one at all!'

Skull in hand, he had unconsciously struck the pensive, ironic pose of Hamlet in the cemetery.

'It was obvious! ...' he finally spoke. 'We ought to have tumbled to this sooner. And yet now, it could have kept us searching for ages! For the last week I've thought of nothing else.'

'Me neither,' admitted Mrs. Blue.

Hippolyte was tossing the skull in his hand.

'What a brain-teaser,' he repeated stupidly, 'what a brain-teaser...! Be fair to me. I've always said that these stories of Gallant, Roussignac, Bertrand and company, they weren't natural.'

'That's true, you've always said that,' agreed Mrs. Blue, looking at him curiously. 'How did you get the idea?'

★ ★ ★

It was ten o'clock the following evening

'Good evening, Mr. Cérisolles,' said Mrs. Blue, 'thanks for having responded to our call.'

The two Blues, brother and sister, were alone at St. Agatha's. She had got the house tidy in anticipation of the meeting they were to have with Mr. Cérisolles, the former manager of the *Wasp-Waist* business. She had sent everyone to the cinema, including Gérard.

Cérisolles had hardly altered; he was simply taller and thinner. And a sad fever burned in his eyes under his increasingly bushy eyebrows, as he looked at the erotic little paintings in the morning room, the Jouy cretonne print, the Louis XV armchairs. This décor was so different from that which he had known when he was selling lingerie.

He had come in hesitantly, with a timid step, with the look of a suspicious old cat. His whole being betrayed a great unease.

'To come back here after all these years... Especially after the grief I've had through the moral lapse of Louise...'

'Ah, let's talk about your wife!' squealed Mrs. Blue. 'Murderer!'

'Excuse me?' Cérisolles was staggered.

The brother and sister had agreed that a brisk attack would be the best option. To leave Cérisolles no time to get his breath.

'Jeanne Roussignac's stove, that was you, hey? And the lorry which ran over Maertens, that was you!'

'The stove? ... The lorry? ...'

'It's pointless putting on this act. We've discovered everything, my good fellow. It's you who stabbed Gallant!'

'Me? ... I stabbed someone? ...'

He looked at them as though they were dangerous lunatics.

'Five crimes! Five crimes to save your neck. To prevent another crime being discovered.'

'You're completely mad!'

'Your wife. Your poor wife...'

'My poor wife? That beats everything. She deceived me and...'

'And you killed her!'

With her fine, fat white hands Mrs. Blue delivered a volley of slaps to Cerisolles.

'You buried her in the cellar!'

Cérisolles, with the look of a hunted man, threw himself towards the door.

'Not so fast...'

Hippolyte Blue had flung himself onto him.

Cérisolles struggled like a maniac, punching and kicking. He was going to knock the weaker Hippolyte down and flee. Mrs. Blue grabbed him by the scruff of his neck with one hand.

'To the cellar! ... To the cellar!'

'But I don't want to go to the cellar,' he shrieked. And he began to shout. 'Help! Help!'

Mrs. Blue's grip pushed him irresistibly into the corridor.

'Aha! You don't want to go to the cellar. Even so, you're going. And we'll see whether you still have the courage to deny it! To the cellar! ... To the cellar!

He stumbled deliberately and fell, hoping to escape the grip of Mrs. Blue. It worked. Immediately he rushed to the end of the corridor, dashed through one room, then another.

The brother and sister were at his heels. He crossed the Marthas' dormitory, then the Marys'. A window was open. He threw himself into the bushes of the Champ-de-Mars, where pursuit would have been in vain.

★ ★ ★

'We're in a fine mess,' Mrs. Blue spoke wearily when she was back in the cellar of bones with her brother.

'How do you mean "mess"? I'm going to the police. And I will give myself the pleasure of seeing him guillotined,' Mr. Blue spoke out savagely.

Mrs. Blue shook her head.

'The trouble is that the police will start by detaining you and me. Even more so because they won't manage straight away to nab Cérisolles. They will question us. They'll grill us. The police do grill those it has detained; it's normal. And they'll charge us!'

'Charge us? With what?'

'For the murder of a person unknown,' Mrs. Blue indicated the skeleton. 'It'll be no use explaining that this is all that remains of poor Mrs. Cérisolles. We won't be able to prove it. And after the business of Maertens, Roussignac, Gallant, Berthault and Bertrand, a skeleton in our cellar, admit it, that takes the biscuit! People will take great pleasure studying closely the "good works" of this institution of charity known as St. Agatha's.'

'Yes, of course,' Blue spoke, realising suddenly that he could in addition be asked personally to account for certain mailings of photographs of young ladies, and for a certain correspondence that he kept going, under number 504, with soldiers stationed in Africa and the Far East, and for certain packages of various value that he received at the Titmouse Agency from these soldiers...

'What are you thinking, little sister?' eventually he asked anxiously.

'I'm thinking that when honest folk discover a skeleton in their cellar...'

'What do they do?'

'They make it disappear,' said Mrs. Blue, 'when they've been idiotic enough to let the murderer get away.'

She poked a finger in his ribs.

'What's keeping you from going and getting Gérard's sidecar out?'

Unconvinced, but finding no weighty argument against his sister, Hippolyte went to remove the machine from a nearby shed. Meanwhile, Mrs. Blue went to get an anonymous piece of cloth from a box of rags, in which to pack the ghoulish debris.

Neither of them remotely suspected that someone was watching them. Aimée had not gone to the cinema, preferring to be tempted, like 'Mr. Seguin's goat', at René de Fouques's despite her resolution not to go again to rue Ravignan. Returning indoors on tiptoe, she had been intrigued by the light in the cellar. She saw the Blues leaning over the skeleton, lost in thought.

As the couple went upstairs, Aimée concealed herself behind a large Breton chest which decorated the entrance, then slipped into the cellar. With her eyes closed, and in horror, she seized the first bone which came to hand. She was in a sort of trance and an absurd word kept passing through her mind – 'Evidence... Evidence...'

The first bone which came to hand was in fact from a hand!

Mrs. Blue returned downstairs, spread out her piece of cloth and began piling the bones at random. Hippolyte came to rejoin her.

'When I think,' he mused, 'that this was a fine-looking girl, delectable!'

'Yes, well, there isn't enough left in here to make a meat broth,' Mrs. Blue threw out cynically. 'And it's not because you are in the Salvation Army that you have to believe you are obliged to philosophise!

'You make me feel sick.' Hippolyte groaned.

He no longer looked the least bit like Hamlet. But Shakespeare's shadow was all the same gliding over them. For this pale, trembling old man and this sniggering female handling these bones in this cellar at dead of night strangely evoked a frightful pair – Macbeth and Lady Macbeth exchanging whispers by the body of Banquo.

Mrs. Blue held up a femur towards the light bulb. It was very clean, well polished and very white.

'There's no doubt about it; death does a proper job.' And she threw the femur back onto the pile in the cloth which she tied at the four corners.

'Where are we going to chuck this? In the Seine?'

'I have a better idea,' mumbled Mr. Blue.

She put the bundle into his arms and again prodded him towards the staircase. Behind the pile of logs, Aimée Laprade squeezed the bony hand in her fleshy one and had to bite her lip not to cry out. For she felt the fingers of the defunct Mrs. Cérisolles breaking up between her fingers. The phalanges came apart as they were only held together by soil.

While Mr. Blue laboured to start Gérard's bike, Mrs. Blue, increasingly like Lady Macbeth although unaware of it, went to wash her muddy fingers under a tap.

Eventually, the diminishing noise of backfiring indicated the motor bike was moving off carrying the Shakespearean couple: Mr. Blue clamped to the handlebars and Mrs. Blue filling up the sidecar with her regal buttocks. Between her feet, in a square of floral cretonne, this small pile of bones which was once 'a fine-looking girl, delectable.'

Aimée Laprade remained alone at the *Protection of the Young Woman*.

★ ★ ★

At the Charentes Hôtel, Red Hands was in bed, contemplating despondently this Laos postage stamp which showed a pretty Indo-Chinese girl with a serious face, almost sad, looking like Mousmé.

Sergeant Besnard... Sergeant Louis Besnard... Red Hands read and reread the name of the soldier who had drawn on his pay to send off an ivory statuette, with his fondest thoughts, to "Miss 504"! He read and reread the postmark. Bangkok... Bangkok – Laos.

Suddenly, a step in the corridor. A knock on the door.

'Mr. Goupi, you're wanted on the telephone.'

Telephone? Red Hands had never used one in his life...! He jumped hurriedly into his trousers.

Who the devil would call him in the middle of the night?

Mousmé possibly... No, that was ridiculous. It could only be little Laprade. He ran into the corridor.

'Hallo, don't hang up,' the night porter spoke with a yawn from a booth, 'I'm passing Mr. Goupi to you.'

Red Hands seized the receiver feverishly.

'Yes, yes... what's up?'

'Hallo! Is that Mr. Red Hands on the phone?'

A woman's voice, not Mousmé, Aimée nor Mrs. Blue.

'Yes, it's me, Red Hands. And you, who are you?'

'My name would not interest you. I only wanted to tell you, if you didn't know, that Miss Aimée Laprade is a slut. She is sleeping with Mr. René de Fouques!'

'You're telling me this!' Red Hands was gob-smacked. 'I'm not her father.'

'What's more,' the voice went on, 'René de Fouques is also Mrs. Blue's lover.'

'What the hell do you think I care!' Red Hands yelled, on the point of adding, 'as for you, you are a nasty little bitch, Miss Agnès Duffeteaux.' For he had recognised the voice. But once more, he judged it absurd to disclose himself. It is so much better when you know and others do not know you know. He restricted himself to repeating,

'Who are you?'

A click, she had hung up.

He spoke again, 'Hallo, Hallo,' because he had noticed that this was done.

Then he left, leaving the receiver dangling on the end of the wire. The night porter, yawning, came to replace it. 'Ah, these peasants! ... '.

Some moments later further knocks on the door, when Red Hands had removed only one leg from his trousers. But this time the knocks were hurried.

'Red Hands? You're there Red Hands? Aimée...'

'One second,' shouted the fellow, distraught.

Already the girl had come in, breathless.

Red Hands hastily thrust his other leg into his trousers, tucked in his day shirt (he wore them as nightshirts when they were sufficiently grubby) and hastily buttoned himself up. He was dreadfully embarrassed when suddenly he saw that Aimée, staring fixedly with her lips trembling, was on the verge of fainting. He grabbed her and sat her down on a chair.

'I'm going to give you a small brandy.'

'No, thank you,' she murmured almost immediately.

She laid a clenched fist on the table.

'Terrible things are going on at St. Agathas,' she said in a gasp. 'I've brought you... this.'

She let roll on to the table a handful of small white objects.

★ ★ ★

Hidden under a porch in Charles Floquet Avenue, the poacher and the solicitor's daughter were watching out.

No light at St. Agatha's; the Blues had not yet returned.

Gérard Blue, Agnès Duffeteaux and the three Marthas were returning from the cinema. The three servant girls were reliving episodes from the film, an American western, and letting out chuckles of rapture.

'Me, the one I liked was the tall fair-haired one, you know the one I'm speaking about, who shot off the end of his friend's cigar with a bullet...'

Behind them, Gérard was relating to Agnès a *Joy of the Beyond* in the saucy style :

Hidden behind some yew trees, two young male skeletons, if I can put it like that, were ogling a group of feisty young female skeletons.

'Ah, I say,' one of the two spoke, 'if we had X-rays we'd see their boobs! ...

Agnès burst out laughing.

When the young man and the girls had shut the door at St. Agatha's, Red Hands spoke to Aimée, 'You go in too. The Blues must not suspect that it's you who caught them in the act. I will tell them I saw them in their cellar. I'll let you know tomorrow what has happened. Until then, you slip off quietly to bed. And not a word, eh?'

They went together into the boarding house.

Passing by the door of the cellar, Aimée shivered, then made off to the Mary's dormitory. She was preparing the lies she was going to have to churn out in reply to the insinuations that the treacherous Agnès would not fail to throw at her.

Meanwhile, Red Hands went down to the cellar and by the light of a match studied the grave. It was shallow and very narrow. Even a small person like Mousmé, with virtually the body of a young girl, must have found it cramped inside. He reflected at length on the graves he had dug, very deep ones, spacious ones, for so many people indifferent to him; even for those he had detested. His jaw tightened.

He remounted the stairs stealthily and slipped into the sitting room containing the erotic miniatures. He sat on a Louis XV armchair, filled his pipe and lit it.

Then, in the gloom and aware of the street noises, as he was to the noises of the forest when lying on the lookout in Goupi country, he began to wait.

★ ★ ★

'I was waiting for you, dear friends,' said Red Hands amiably. 'You'll forgive me, I took the liberty of switching on the electric light, at the risk of burning myself.'

On hearing the motor bike arriving, he had indeed put the light on to signal his presence. Now, with his left hand he was tapping the bowl of his pipe against an ashtray. But the Blues were watching his right hand that he kept deep in his jacket pocket. They were thinking that it held a pistol.

Hippolyte felt a thread of cold sweat trickle the length of his spine and Mrs. Blue was unable to control a trembling which had seized hold of her knees.

'I know very well that this is no time for visiting people but a peasant has been rather dragged up hasn't he? You see, I came across a good skeleton tale and said to myself "I must make my Blue friends benefit from it because they are so kind to me, and they've been so good to Aimée... and Mousmé."

Hippolyte leaned against a table. With one hand he nervously tugged his beard, leaving hairs between his fingers.

Mrs. Blue had sat down, those knees knocking under her dress; this was intolerable.

'What does this mean? She growled.

'I don't believe that your son will find my story good enough to put in his book. But it will surely amuse you. This happens in a cemetery of course.

A young skeleton approaches an old skeleton who is wearing a shroud; one with a pocket! "Young man," says the old skeleton, "I bet you are coming to ask me for my daughter's hand." The young skeleton says "Exactly." The elder speaks "I grant it to you. In fact, it's in my pocket. Here. Take it."'

At the same time Red Hands put the bones on a table.

'What's this?'

'Oh, a small thing. "There wouldn't be enough to make a meat broth." It's only a hand – well actually what's left of it! But all the bones are there, you can check. And what's better, it's the hand of a woman!'

His voice changed.

'It's the hand of my niece Mousmé, whom you murdered and buried in your cellar two years ago.'

He kept on the alert, expecting them to pounce on him or rush off.

Instead the pair of them stared at each other, dumbfounded.

Then Mr. Blue made this extraordinary comment:

'This is not going to be easy to explain to him.'

He had to start at the beginning.

Cérisolles, deceived and then abandoned by his young wife. A commonplace tale, touching and somewhat ridiculous. The cuckold, who is unable to get over it, is continuing to live alone in the place where everything recalls the act of betrayal. He hands his business over to the Blues, sells it for peanuts, disposes of it as if running away from something.

Then, a series of dramas. These names which ended up sounding like an idiotic litany – Maertens, Roussignac, Gallant, Berthault, Bertrand...

A string of coincidences? An unbelievable whodunnit? No! Crimes!

Crimes committed by Cérisolles, prepared to do anything to prevent the discovery that he had murdered and buried his wife in the cellar.

★ ★ ★

They had left the morning room.

Somewhat shame-faced, Red Hands had agreed to follow them to the pantry.

Salami, oysters, white Moselle.

'You won't mind if we have a snack informally in the kitchen?' Mrs. Blue had enquired.

Red Hands did not use the oyster fork; he opened the oysters with the point of his pocket knife. Not without difficulty he divided each oyster into two, making two mouthfuls.

'Why? Why?' He repeated.

'Cérisolles kills his wife and buries her. Fine. She no longer had any living relatives. No-one to worry about her, to make enquiries, to lodge a complaint. Except the lover, but he believed she had gone off with someone else.

Everyone is sorry for Cérisolles, while he plays the rôle of the inconsolable cuckold. Everyone understands the 'poor man', when he puts his shop up for sale under the pretext that the sorrow, the loneliness...'

In reality, he could no longer bear to spend time in the shop because his wife was there, right there in the cellar!

'Right then! So he sells up. Up until then it's all plain sailing. But the other crimes? Why has Cérisolles acted as though he absolutely depended on preventing your selling up? As though you yourselves weren't the problem – whereas others would have made him anxious?'

'You've hit the nail on the head,' Mrs. Blue spoke. 'He was afraid of those who wanted to replace us!'

'For what reason?'

'A childish one!'

'For all that,' cut in Hippolyte, 'both of us, my sister and I, have had the devil of a job finding her. I found her first.' He puffed himself up and poured some white wine.

Mrs. Blue discarded the oyster shells, changed the plates, and served half a cold chicken and a ripe Camembert.

'Luxury!' She said. 'Cérisolles killed the others because they wanted to set up luxury businesses.'

'Look here,' said Red Hands, 'you're not going to tell me that Cérisolles hated flowers, music, pretty paintings, lap dogs, luxury birds and luxury fish to the point of going to kill all those who...'

'Exactly,' said Mrs. Blue.

'To take in some ten young ladies fallen from the nest, there is no need for complicated living arrangements. These young ladies can do without space, light and even air at a pinch.'

But a lot of air, light and space must be available for displaying painted canvasses, for showing off in cages or aquaria, lap dogs, luxury birds, luxury fish, for the tasteful arrangement of flowers, luxuriant plants, greenery, and for lining up long rows of musical boxes.

'To set up my boarding house,' continued Mrs. Blue, 'I had no need to get major changes done on the house. So there was almost no chance that I ever come across the body of Mrs. Cérisolles. But those people, who intended to buy up my lease would have been obliged, by the nature of their business, to have these alterations done. Consequently, they would almost certainly have come across the skeleton. Cérisolle's neck was at risk!'

Red Hands shut his pocket knife, thanked them for the excellent supper and apologised again.

'You are not too annoyed with me for having suspected you?'

'Come, come Mr. Red Hands! No need to apologise!'

'I can fill in the hole if you like,' he proposed this to gain forgiveness.

'Don't think of it,' Mrs. Blue protested, 'we will do that ourselves very well' … she smiled… 'less well than you of course, Mr. Red Hands!'

'Come on, don't fuss! Give me a shovel and I'll fill it in two ticks. A trifle of a hole. I know this, it's my job.'

So there they were in the cellar. There was Red Hands slipping off his jacket and grabbing the shovel. There the hole was filled, the soil compacted and smoothed well.

'Thank you so much dear Mr. Red Hands,' simpered Mrs. Blue.

'It's nothing, dear Mrs. Blue.' Red Hands assured her, rolling the bones in his pocket between his fingers.

'By the way,' he enquired perversely, 'where the devil did you get rid of the skeleton?'

'At the Flea Market! Mr. Blue replied. 'I hung the bundle on the shutter of an antique shop.'

'Joker!'

They parted, wishing each other goodnight. And the Blues, standing at their front door, laughed good-heartedly when Red Hands turned to shout at them :

'Don't have any bad dreams!'

CHAPTER 11

HAND GAMES

Left side, right side, on the stomach, on the back, in the foetal position; nothing worked. Red Hands could not get to sleep.

He could not stop working out in his brain the bones which make up the hand – in his capacity of a quack doctor he knew them well.

'The eight small ones of the wrist. The five connecting bones of the palm. Eight and five are thirteen. The five proximal finger bones; thirteen and five – eighteen. The next five bones; eighteen and five – twenty-three. Only four end finger bones, making twenty-seven.'

More tossing about. And the stupid squirrelling work of insomnia, which started off again.

'The eight small bones of the wrist, the five conecting metacarpal bones. Eight and five – thirteen...'

He groaned. He puffed.

'The five middle bones... eighteen and five...'

He tossed and turned. He sweated.

'Only four end finger bones. Twenty-three and four...'

Think of something else... Think of something else...

Now he was lining up one after the other expressions containing the word 'hand'.

Raising a hand, clapping hands, forcing one's hand, coming to fisticuffs, hands up, put up a hand, winning hands down, hands down, lay hands on, light-handedly, put one's hand to it, hands tied, first hand, putting the finishing touches to, to wash one's hand of it, to be in good hands, hole in the hand, hands full, hand on heart, open-handed, bone idle, hand on face, hands to the pumps, hand on bum, what fills the hand of an honest man, to the innocents full hands...

These hands – like a swarm of spiders.

Helping hand, armed hand, from the master's hand, it's only your hand, Madam, hands game, sleight of hand, tiny hand, flat of the hand, the hand of cards moves on, business in hand, handrail, handful of paper, hired hand, black-hand gang, red-handed, criminal hand, cut my hand off on it, my hand in the fire on it, the left hand does not know, hand sports, lines of the hand, hand of glory, the Graces' hand, Fatima's hand, my sister's hand...

And always, over this cascade of hands, the bony one of Mrs. Cérisolles, and the fluttering, marvellous fat white hands of Mrs. Blue.

Exasperated, Red Hands got up, pulled on his trousers and without thinking began to arrange the twenty-seven small bones.

He went off to ask the night porter for a sheet of paper and a pencil.

Then, transferring the hand on to the paper, he drew a line round it, taking care to leave a space between the bones and the pencil line to indicate flesh.

This hand, like a flower! Red Hands pondered on Louise Cérisolles with her nimble fingers which, after gently fitting corsets or bras, rested softly on the hair of a lover, and strayed slowly over his eyes and mouth...

It was the right hand, the one for love-making. Red Hands asked himself whether it is to make the betrayal less cruel, less unholy, that one wears one's wedding ring on the left hand?

Then, totally surprised to have had such an idea, he went angrily to empty his bladder via the window into the street. He got back into bed with the determined will to sleep.

★ ★ ★

Brother and sister Blue at St. Agatha's did not sleep either.

Nor Agnès. She bit the pillow to choke back tears of rage...

A little earlier, Aimée Laprade, haunted by the skeleton in the cave, and not daring to drop off to sleep, had quietly got up, opened the window, and leaned out to fill her lungs with the fresh night air.

A voice called to her, softly. Gérard, leant out of his bedroom window on the first floor. He was calling to her, smiling with signs meaning 'Come and join me.'

At any other time, at the idea of finding herself alone with a young man in the middle of the night two steps from a bed, and Aimée would have shrugged her shoulders with distaste.

But this was a night so charged with fear, so filled with wild ideas.

And then, Gérard was not like the others. Close to him there was no question of thinking of anything at all. You watched him, listened to him, and laughed.

Even the grins of skeletons became smiles!

Aimée had crossed the dormitory softly so as not to wake Agnès.

But Agnès had followed her and seen her go into the young man's bedroom.

★ ★ ★

'A solicitor's office, what is it? The archives of a cemetery, nothing more nor less. What is to be found in the binders? Wills! Records of inheritance, legacies, annuities. What are euphemistically called 'expectations'. The saddest of associations – money and death!'

Aimée and the adolescent Gérard were sitting on his bed both in their dressing gowns. Gérard had undertaken to explain to her why she had escaped from her father's home.

'The death of some means money for others! And not

only money! There is the furniture. The linen. The pots and pans. All these objects that will be shared out with the courtesy of wolves dividing a carcass!'

He offered her a cigarette.

She declined; she had never smoked before.

'Take it!' he said. 'That's an order!'

In this way did Aimée make the acquaintance of tobacco that night.

'There is also the *land*,' he continued. 'The fields, enclosed by walls, by fences, by trellises. The ground, reduced to numbered plots.'

'Plots, savour this word, Aimée. "When the ancient cousin kicks the bucket, I'll have his plot 38 and his plot 51." It's because of all this that your father's house is making you think of a cemetery. It's dead simple! It's the reason you left. And you were dead right!'

They smiled to each other.

'You must understand,' he said, 'why I like skeletons so much. Skeletons are totally straightforward. They envy no-one, they have no expectations and nothing to bequeath. They're as innocent as a new-born baby.'

They lit another cigarette. Gérard then resumed in a hesitant voice :

'Relevant to this, I have a cemetery story that I like best of all, but I won't put it in my book because people wouldn't understand it. But I'd like to know if you like it.':

A young male skeleton cuddles a young female skeleton. The female murmurs "My love, when you hold me like this in your arms I'm so happy I could die."

It's stupid isn't it?

Aimée smiled at him without responding.

For a while they remained quiet.

And it was on this night that Gérard Blue finally dared to confess to Aimée Laprade that he loved her.

★ ★ ★

Next morning Red Hands launched himself bravely and alone towards the darkest regions of the remote eighteenth district. When taking the Métro, he no longer requested a ticket to travel to the end of the line. He knew that the travellers who presented a reference number to the bus conductors were not season-ticket holders. The traffic policemen no longer impressed him, nor the cars. He was not put out by pedestrian crossings. He was becoming a true Parisian.

At 28 rue Boinod, close to boulevard Ornano, deep in the eighteenth district, he asked for Mr. Jean Cérisolles.

'Second floor on the right.'

He had only come to make sure. He was not a policeman and the Cérisolles affair did not concern him. Needless to say, there was no Cérisolles on the second floor.

Red Hands took himself to the Flea Market – still just to make sure. The Goupi family follows to the very end everything they undertake. In any case, he wasn't far from Porte de Clignancourt. He went there on foot.

Hippolyte Blue had not mentioned the name of the trader on whose shutters he had hung the grisly package. But it could only be the antique dealer to whom he sold his trash from the Far East.

In fact, Red Hands had only to ask 'You wouldn't have come across a package when you opened your stall this morning?', blowing into the stem of his pipe and adding casually, 'a suspect package...' He saw the fellow blanch.

'Yes, Inspector!'

"Inspector" Red Hands!

'A skeleton, eh?'

'Yes, Inspector.'

'What have you done with it?'

'Inspector, I thought it was a joke. So I went and left the package in the front of the shop of a colleague.' He mentioned the name and place.

'You didn't think it was a joke. You thought of foul play and said to yourself "I don't want trouble."'

'The thing is, Inspector...'

But already Red Hands had moved off in the direction indicated.

At the second store it was the same. There again they called him Inspector.

'It's true, Inspector... without a doubt I've done wrong. I ought to have gone to the police. But I thought it was a hoax, you know... I was afraid of disturbing these gentlemen for nothing...'

The second trader had left the package in front of the shop of a third shopkeeper.

Along the passageways, where already a number of shoppers were nosing about, this skeleton hunt was taking on a vaudeville atmosphere.

Following with an anxious look the ponderous figure of Red Hands, each of the traders interrogated was filled with wonder. 'It's fantastic, he's managed to look like a peasant. You would have said he still has mud on his boots. You can go on taking the mickey out of them but these CID characters are incredibly crafty!'

The third trader had hastened to rid himself of the compromising parcel by surreptitiously leaving it in front of the shop of a fourth colleague!

A nursery rhyme was running through Red Hands' head

He runs, he runs, the ferret,
the ferret of the woods, ladies...

The investigation came to an end in a small restaurant right in the heart of the Flea Market.

A cheerful redhead was preparing chickens for the lunchtime meal. She would have still been attractive if she had bothered to struggle against putting on weight.

As Red Hands began to speak, she burst out:

'Less than ten minutes ago the boss took that blasted parcel to the police station and you're here already! ...Then the light dawned. 'How stupid of me. You met him?'

'No, I don't know him.'

'Then how could you...'

'It's my job to know.'

It was she who had found the package in the dustbin on opening the restaurant.

'The boss thought it was a joke. Me, I told him "It's a crime, I'm sure it's a crime." It really is a crime, isn't it, Inspector?'

'It's a crime, Madame.'

Suddenly, he realised that by hanging about there longer he risked getting into trouble. The police would want to know what whim had persuaded him to adopt the title of Inspector. He would have to tell the tale of Mousmé, the Blue family, their cellar, Cérisolles and his rosary of infamies – Maertens, Roussignac, Gallant, Berthault, Bertrand... A thousand worries in prospect!

'I'm coming back shortly,' he told the woman, who insisted on showing him the dustbin.

'D'you believe that they'll succeed in identifying the victim? That's not going to be easy, eh?'

'We already know, she's a certain Louise Cérisolles.'

'What! ...' She had had a shock.

'You knew her?'

Instead of answering, she asked, 'What did she do, in her work?'

'Corset maker. She kept a shop "The Wasp Waist", avenue Charles Floquet. She was murdered by her husband Jean Cérisolles because she was unfaithful to him. He had buried her in his cellar.'

The woman was obliged to sit down, bent in two by a sudden fit of laughing. She hiccoughed. 'Louise Cérisolles of "The Wasp Waist" – is me! As for deceiving my husband Jean, yes I certainly did deceive him. But as to having been murdered by him and buried in the cellar, well I never, well I never...

'The Blues have had me, and really had me!' Red Hands was dumbfounded.

He clenched his fists. 'How can I have been so stupid not to guess? That small hand... so very tiny. And Mousmé, hardly bigger than a young girl! Her narrow shoulders, those thin wrists... like most Indo-Chinese.'

'In the cellar! Buried in the cellar! … ,' the woman spluttered, convulsed with laughter. Red Hands sneaked away without her noticing.

Flushed, and with tears of laughter, she stuttered 'I'm peeing myself! … Oh dear, … I'm doing a wee!'

CHAPTER 12

'INSPECTOR' RED HANDS

The apartment building number 14 in the rue Du Dragon was cracked and blackish, the stairway steep with peeling walls. It was no longer a staircase as such between the fourth and fifth floors, it became a sort of wooden step ladder.

A corridor of maid's rooms with the walls and doors the colour of faeces. The doors were numbered. At the end of the corridor, a water tap and toilet with old newspapers scattered around. The latch was broken and the door stayed permanently open.

Girls with faces of incurable imbecility glazed with a cream, and framed with bundles of hair – slaves' faces – were appearing, in sordid dressing-gowns disclosing low unsupported breasts and legs criss-crossed with varicose veins. They fetched water in dented jugs. One younger girl came out from Room 8 humming and dancing. A refreshing miracle! A pixie fulfilling her purgatory time on earth!

The lace of an absinthe green georgette slip fluttered on her blooming breasts and her twinkling legs. Shutting herself in the lavatory and still humming, she took a close look at Red Hands through a chink in the door. What was this fellow with a moustache and with this strange hat on his head doing at the top of the stairs? A copper surely?

A little earlier Red Hands had seen Hippolyte Blue entering the Titmouse Private Post then re-emerging laden with small parcels and taking the route to rue Du Dragon.

It was no longer the moment to consider expense, Red Hands had jumped into a taxi.

And now he was hearing this old rascal Hippolyte Blue coming up the stairs.

To conceal himself, Red Hands had no choice and took the place of the pixie with the absinthe green slip, in the wc. He saw Hippolyte go into Room 7 and he spied through the keyhole.

It was a pokey attic, nine feet by six; with a skylight in the ceiling. A cane armchair and a small office desk with drawers made up the furniture. The desk had a glass, a bottle of Pernod, a carafe, a clay pot full of tobacco and an ashtray. The wardrobe comprised a pair of slippers lined with lamb's wool and, hanging from a nail, a large quilted Japanese kimono of azure blue embellished with golden dragons.

In addition, there was a small electric radiator and, in a corner on a newspaper some thirty books piled up. Big de luxe books covered with transparent paper.

Hippolyte Blue began by opening the packages brought from the Titmouse Private Post. A scarf, an amber necklace, sculpted ivory plates, and so on.

He slipped on his fur-lined slippers and the quilted kimono.

Then, taking the glass and carafe, trotted over towards the door. At the tap in the corridor, he rinsed the glass and filled the carafe with the careful actions of a grandee. He returned to his room.

Red Hands, eye at the keyhole, was obliged to hold his opera hat in his hand, which bothered him.

Blue had plugged in the radiator and put half a dozen books on the table. He filled his pipe, lit it, prepared himself a Pernod, drank a mouthful, opened a book and immersed himself in the study of an engraving.

Red Hands was going to knock when Blue quickly raised his head. He stood up and slipped towards a wall where he remained motionless. From his observation post Red Hands could not decipher the reason for this move.

He put on his hat and knocked. At the sight of him all the colour drained from Blue's face.

Red Hands went straightaway on the offensive.

'Pretty, that kimono. Is it a sergeant who sent it to you? Or a corporal? To the Titmouse Private Post as usual? Box 504...That's so practical.'

He had spoken softly. The partition walls had no more than three fingers of thickness and in adjacent rooms, the slightest noise of a jug or a basin, and each step of the girls was audible.

He pushed Hippolyte out of the way, shut the door and lightly touched with his foot the objects from the Far East, saying ironically:

'Exotics! More exotics! Always exotics! And France will be saved, as they say, at the Flea Market.'

Blue was quaking at the knees.

'Sit yourself down,' Red Hands spoke. 'You're at home.'

In a desk drawer he found a fountain pen, a bottle of ink, stamps, writing paper and envelopes. In another, a collection of colonial newspapers with some advertisements ticked. In a third drawer, an address book and photographs of young ladies – the boarders at St. Agatha's, the three skivvies, Agnès Duffeteaux, Aimée Laprade and some others Red Hands did not know. The address book contained the names of soldiers, from private up to lieutenant, stationed in French overseas garrisons.

Under each name Blue had written another, strange and poetic:

Wild Pansy, Cornflower, Silver Star, Snowdrop, Bleeding Heart, April Shower.

'The example of that serial killer Landru ought to have served as a lesson to you?' said Red Hands, still in a low voice. It was a notebook which got him caught. Of course, one needs book-keeping, order and method, but not more than necessary.'

He leafed through the notebook, coming back to the first pages.

'There!' he spoke abruptly, putting his forefinger on a name:

'Brother. Pnom-Penh.'

Under the name he underlined another:

'Colibri.'

He went to hang his hat on the nail which served to hang the kimono, then pulled from his wallet the old, yellowed and creased photograph of his great niece.

'Photograph of Miss Mousmé, known as "Colibri", taken in the art studio of master photographer Hippolyte Blue, avenue Charles Floquet! Agreed?'

Blue nodded pitifully.

'So?' Red Hands spoke.

'So what? You know everything.'

'What became of Colibri?'

Sticking to his method of keeping back his trump card, Red Hands had decided not to breathe a word about his meeting with Louise Cérisolles in the Flea Market restaurant.

'But we did nothing to Colibri,' Blue protested plaintively, 'we did her only good. And one morning she left us, without a word, not a thank you, like an ungrateful child.'

'Very well,' said Red Hands tapping the address book, 'I'm curious to know what the long arm of the law will think of your goings on at the Titmouse Private Post. Not to mention your Salvation Army card and the "Lady of the Stations!"'

Blue had a horrible fear of the police. But there was someone of whom he had an even greater fear – his sister Agatha Blue.

'I'll give you interesting information if you promise not to speak of this business of the letters to my sister.'

'I have no promise to make to you!'

'Of course,' admitted Blue, 'I trust to your good heart. I swear to you that neither my sister nor I know what has become of Colibri. But René de Fouques probably knows. He was her lover.'

'Ah! ... her too?'

'But all of them as and when they pass through St. Agatha's!' Blue said with a limp gesture. 'Well, all of them that aren't too ugly. That Don Juan is insatiable... and my sister is the only one not to realise it! So René had uncovered my "goings-on" as you call them and me, I had discovered his. He had me in a grip but I had him too. So there... I've told you everything I know. Really everything.'

He opened a fourth drawer; it was stuffed with paper, letters from the soldiers in the colonies! 'In reality, I wasn't doing such a bad thing,' he pleaded in a whining tone. 'These soldiers, in far-flung countries and feeling homesick; it gave them such pleasure getting letters from young ladies, replying, sending little gifts...'

'You were improving army moral. Really patriotic work!'

'Don't exaggerate! I'm not thinking of asking for the Legion d'Honneur. And me,' he concluded, 'I made a bit of money from the gifts. That's because my sister is greedy. She's full of René! "Her" René! She gives him everything, me nothing. Nevertheless, I need a bit of pocket money to lead a decent life as a bachelor'!

Red Hands took two or three books from the desk.

Erotic works, copiously illustrated. It was on these purchases that the money went, which the fine fellow got from his trips to the Flea Market!

'It's not going too far, you know', said Hippolyte. 'It's hardly wicked!'

An impulse drove Red Hands towards the wall near where earlier he had seen Hippolyte through the keyhole, incomprehensibly standing still.

Straight away he cottoned on. A hole the size of a pea in the thin partition.

A glance through this hole revealed Room 8, that of the young lady in the absinthe green slip.

She was busy washing combs in a basin. Red Hands

had a frontal view of her; a child, sixteen at the most. Pretty but above all fresh looking. An innocent face and big blue eyes. Red Hands saw her practically naked. Flesh-coloured stockings, attached to a narrow suspender belt, absinthe green knickers and a bra of the same colour.

'To enjoy a bachelor's life!'

Passing his dirty look over this child in bloom, after having dragged it through his books, then caressing a nasty fantasy while sipping his glass of pernod and sucking his pipe – this is what Hippolyte Blue, in his mandarin kimono, called 'enjoying a bachelor's life!'

Suddenly, Red Hands had a sharp intake of breath. The tip of his shoe had grated with the faintest noise against the skirting board. Nevertheless, the girl had heard it and immediately her look went towards the wall. But not, as expected, in the direction of the skirting board from where the sound had come. She looked straight towards the hole, exactly at the height of the hole and surprisingly, her look had no sign of anxiety, nor even, at least, of perplexity. And the strangest thing, this unambiguous look, direct, and sharp as a needle, was instantly turned away. Red Hands even thought he detected a smile on the angelic face. The hint of a smile, as sharp as the look.

No! It wasn't possible! Red Hands must have deceived himself. He really wished he was deceived... that what he had taken for a smile was no more than a twitch of her lips.

Well, not so. He had not deceived himself!

He saw the girl let her combs sink to the bottom of the basin and dry her hands. She passed them behind her back. Not looking at the hole, she placed herself facing the wall. Slowly she raised her hands behind her back. Slowly they met the straps of her bra, which slipped a little. Calculated slowness... then the bra slid down completely.

'The dirty little trollop,' reflected Red Hands.

One thing was clear... she knew.

She knew that her neighbour, the old figure in the

Japanese kimono, spent his time spying on her through the hole in the wall! And she went along with this game.

Now her hands slid towards her hips...

Red Hands withdrew abruptly, his face crimson with shame, as if the girl had been able to see him!

At his desk Blue, pipe and Pernod in hand, was gazing at Red Hands with a bawdy look.

On the steps of the sordid stairway, in the dilapidated rue du Dragon, on the elegant boulevard St Germain, and even in the Métro which took him towards the Montmartre heights, Red Hands wanted to press his hands over his eyes to chase away the vision which pursued him – this face of a brazen angel above those young breasts shy as the coming of Spring.

★ ★ ★

The low table was made of a long plate of engraved mirror in the Venetian style. Set on this was a piece of genuine Dresden china, a large illustrated edition of Jean Giraudoux's *Suzanne and the Pacific*, Parma violets in a crystal glass flute, and a sheet of de luxe notepaper – pure Auvergne linen – which carried some lines in pencil. "A suggestive story to propose to that cretin Gérard":

Two old female skeletons, wearing shrouds dropping down to their ankles, watch reprovingly a group of young female skeletons also in shrouds but revealing their shins. One of the two old skeletons is grumbling:

'With this new fashion they'll end up by showing their backsides!'

Red Hands had hung his hat unaffectedly on the iron fist of the Middle-Age armour in which, long ago, Gonzague de Fouques had fought, cut and thrust 'for God, for Mary and the King.'

'You were the lover of Colibri,' said Red Hands. 'You know what became of her. If you won't say anything, I'll break your neck.'

A cigarette with a filter tip between his lips, perfumed with 'Russian Leather', marvellously suave and frail-looking in a puffy, monogrammed black silk shirt, the daintiest grey corduroy trousers, and balancing negligently on the end of his right foot a satin slipper in silver brocade, René de Fouques was unmoved.

'I am giving you a kindly warning. If you make a movement I have only to open this drawer to take out a revolver and shoot you before you've had time to get round this armchair. You introduce yourself to my home and make death threats. Self-defence. I will be acquitted and that will give me good publicity into the bargain.'

He let out a few smoke rings.

'I wish you no harm, my good farmer, but we are not in the woods here. As for Colibri, she was the most charming of girlfriends – pretty, a divine figure and, what is better than anything, what is invaluable – reticent, quiet...'

Frowning, Red Hands reflected on the skeleton in the cellar.

'In short,' continued René, ' she left me a charming memory of her and I hope that nothing regrettable has happened to her. But I swear to you that I have absolutely no idea what became of her.'

He looked directly at Red Hands.

'I know you detest me. You have a horror of the type of man that I am. That's normal. We are too different and everything separates us. I regret that.'

Red Hands gave a slight start and fiddled with his pipe to regain his composure.

René mistook the gesture.

'You may smoke your pipe if you wish. The smell does not disturb me. Agatha smokes a pipe when she honours me with her visits. Agatha, that's Mrs. Blue,' he specified.

He rose, went to pat an aquarium and rattle the bars of a cage. He thought no more of the revolver. And in the still serious voice, he continued:

'Yes, I regret that you have an aversion for me. Because personally, I have a liking for you.'

He gave a light laugh.

'Yes, however odd that may seem to you ... you make me think of a big, good animal. A little fierce but with a good big heart deep down eager for affection. Myself, I play the puppet. It's a reliable way to succeed quickly here without trouble and without tiring oneself. Paris loves to give itself puppets for kings, marionettes. But do me the honour of not taking me for an idiot. I'd like to help you, honestly. If you promise me not to tell Mrs. Blue of my "infidelities", I will give you information which can be useful to you, perhaps ...'

The situation took the same turn as with Hippolyte Blue. René and Hippolyte had one feature in common – their fear of Mrs. Blue!

'I can promise you nothing,' Red Hands spoke haughtily.

'Ah! It's clear you come from the Danube.'

'From the Danube?'

'Don't try to understand. It's a literary allusion.'

He found himself near the piano. Dreamily he brushed a few keys.

'In the end, you can say what you like to Agatha. You will do a bad thing; you will break her heart. So much the worse. You will only bring forward the time for tears. Because, so far as I'm concerned, I'm a little weary of this comedy, and...'

The studio gleamed in the sun. The fish became golden fish, the birds golden birds.

'It's not a disagreeable spot here,' he spoke flippantly. 'But one must not grow attached. I'm tempted by a long journey... America... South America of course. Don't speak to me of North America, that country of gum-chewing muscle men. Left to chew something, I prefer coca!'

'You are considering taking Aimée with you?'

René had a lofty smile. 'Don Juan travels light. And

besides, this gentle child attaches excessive importance to her virginity. In a sense, moreover, this is what makes her more interesting. Interesting but boring.'

Red Hands stood up.

'You were going to give me some information about Colibri?'

'Ah, yes. The last time I saw her was here, some two years ago, and the little fool revealed to me she was four months pregnant. One can't imagine it! ... She hadn't dared to tell me.'

'And what did you say? ...'

'That I did not feel myself in the rôle of father of a family. Oh, I told her with every possible kindness. I wiped her beautiful eyes, full of tears. She was smiling when she left. Well, almost smiling.'

'How long before she disappeared from St. Agatha's did that happen?'

'Three days exactly. I give you my word that since then I have not had the least news.'

Red Hands got up again:

'I am a gravedigger but it would not amuse me to bury you,' he spoke coldly. 'It's dreadful just how much you stink when alive. What will it be like when you are dead?'

CHAPTER 13

BLOOD FOR SUPPER

A cemetery somewhere in Africa. A negro cemetery naturally! A negro skeleton...

Mrs. Blue, Hippolyte, Gérard and René de Fouques were taking coffee in the sitting room of St. Agatha's.

They jumped.

Red Hands came in, accompanied by a young Indo-Chinese lady in national dress.

'You have found Colibri?' Hippolyte, Gérard and René exlaimed together.

But Mrs. Blue's look jumped from the dress to the girl's face; she saw clearly it was not Colibri.

'Who's this?' she asked.

Red Hands had had the opportunity of chatting with this young lady in the Latin Quarter. She thought she had known Colibri, although some time ago. However, she was not certain about it.

Red Hands took her to St. Agatha's in the hope that Colibri, if it was indeed Colibri that she had known, had shown her the boarding house.

Sadly the girl shook her head.

'I never came here. I must have got the wrong person.'

Mrs. Blue invited her as well as Red Hands to take coffee.

Four days had gone by since Red Hand's visit to the room in rue Du Dragon and to the studio in rue Ravignan. Hippolyte and René privately regarded Red Hands with gratitude, for he had not revealed to Mrs. Blue either the senile pleasures of her brother, or the infidelity of her lover.

'You were telling one of your *Gaieties from the Beyond*?' he said to Gérard.

'It's a racist story,' said the young man:

A cemetery somewhere in Africa. A negro cemetery of course. A skeleton of a Negro looks at himself in the mirror and murmurs rapturously – "White at last!"

★ ★ ★

In the Marys' dormitory at St. Agatha's, Agnès was having an hysterical outburst in front of Aimée. Tears, abuse, pleas and stifled cries. Not daring to throw herself on her friend, she was scratching at herself; her nails tracing reddish stripes on her whitish yellow chest and her already insignificant breast.

'I love René! I love him, do you understand? And you have stolen him from me! I went and rang on his bell; I'm certain he was there. He didn't open up. When he comes here he avoids me. If I succeed in being alone with him he kisses me only because he can't do otherwise. I feel that I weary him. If you hadn't come here with your hypocritical saintly airs, he would still be mine. We were due to go away together. You have stolen him from me but I will defend myself; I'm capable of anything. If only you loved him... But you don't know what love is. You're just a lecher! When you leave the arms of René it's to run to those of Gérard. Because I've seen you, you know! At night you go and join Gérard in his bedroom.'

'I forbid you to speak Gérard's name,' Aimée spoke fiercely. 'First of all, there has been nothing between Gérard and me! Oh! I don't really care that you don't believe me. And as for René, I'd rather throw myself in the Seine than let myself be kissed by him! ... That too, you don't believe! That someone can go to a fellow's bedroom without lying in his bed, that's beyond you! You're petty! You're cheap! You enjoy yourself only among smutty things. And you're jealous... Jealous... Jealous even of other people's shadows. But it's the truth. Your René gives me the creeps. The creeps...!

She laughed scornfully.

'"Your" René! As though he was yours! I haven't taken him from you, it's he that has lost interest in you! You would like to keep him, you poor lunatic! But it's he who didn't want to keep you. What amuses him is corrupting. He rejected you – as he has discarded the others before you – when he had corrupted you!'

'Corrupted?'

'Yes, obviously it's difficult corrupting you!'

Agnés was humbling herself. 'You are pretty; you please them all. So, you don't understand.' She went in front of the mirror and studied her features with revulsion.

'I'm ugly... ugly... I have a mouth like a knife slit... little eyes... bad skin. But just the same René still fancied me. With René I had a chance.'

She was sobbing.

'My only chance.'

She grabbed at an obscure hope.

'Is it really true that René gives you the creeps? You're not saying it to please me? It's true?'

She was sickening! ...

'It's true,' said Aimée. 'And I'll tell him. I'll throw it full in his face!'

★ ★ ★

Red Hands took the young Indo-Chinese lady back as far as the La Motte-Picquet Métro station.

'Are you satisfied?' she asked.

'Very satisfied,' he spoke in a serious tone, 'you have done me a good turn.'

He wanted to give her a five hundred franc note but she refused it.

'I'm happy if I've been useful to you.' With a kind smile she added: 'To you and to a compatriot... I hope you find her.'

He took his leave, raising his 1830 policeman's hat on high.

★ ★ ★

'Would you have some onions?' Red Hands enquired of Mrs. Blue the next evening. She passed him a basket over which drifted smells of onions, garlic heads, shallots, tarragon, chives, bay, chervil, parsley, peppercorns, thyme and cloves, blended into a sort of modest and touching evocation of a small vegetable garden.

Red Hands attacked an onion with his pocket knife and started to cut it into small pieces, shutting his eyes to stop them watering.

He had arrived at the boarding house in high spirits. Mysteriously, he had taken Mrs. Blue along to the kitchen:

'I've brought you something nice to eat!'

He had shown her a bottle full of thick reddish liquid.

'What is it?'

'Blood!'

'What!'

'Pig's blood! It's my friend at La Villette who gave it to me. I'm thinking of leaving tomorrow for home. You've looked after me so well that before leaving you I'd be happy to get you to taste a dish from my part of the world. It's Goupi grub!'

Under the amused eye of Mrs. Blue he was browning the onions in a frying pan on the gas stove.

She had taken in only one thing; tomorrow he was off, they were going to be free of his obsessive presence.

'My investigation is complete.' He stirred the onions with the point of his knife. 'It was nasty work but it had to be done.'

'Your investigation is finished?'

'Colibri is dead. Pass the bottle of blood will you?'

He poured the pig's blood into the frying pan and continued stirring with the point of his knife.

'Dead and buried, no mistake about that.' He sniggered gloomily. 'I know who killed her.'

He added small cubes of fatty bacon, tarragon and seasoning. As it cooked the blood solidified into lumps.

One of the Marthas appeared at the kitchen door.

'There's a lady here who'd like to speak to Mr. Red Hands. She didn't want to give her name.'

'I know who it is,' said Red Hands. Then, to Mrs. Blue:

'I've taken the liberty of meeting her here. I would have picked an earlier time but she's working. You don't mind?'

'That's all right! ...' Mrs. Blue was alarmed.

'Bring the lady here,' ordered Red Hands to the Martha.

'In the kitchen!' protested Mrs. Blue.

'Pooh! I don't stand on ceremony with her!'

The visitor was ginger-haired, plump and chirpy. She examined everything with interest.

'This gives me an odd feeling, finding myself here,' she exclaimed. 'You've changed everything in the kitchen... It's true that it's a boarding house, bound to be so... my poor cuckold of a husband and I, there were only the two of us...'

'But who are you?' asked Mrs. Blue.

'Louise Cérisolles. It's me that leased *The Wasp Waist*. At the moment, I'm in a restaurant in the Flea Market.'

'Yes, yes,' said Red Hands. 'she's really alive. Her bones are firmly fixed together, as you can notice.'

'And I hope,' he added good-naturedly,' that a great deal more water will pass under the bridge before Mrs. Cérisolles becomes a skeleton!'

'Bravo!' Mrs. Blue's only response.

'And business? It goes well? You are happy?' asked Mrs. Cérisolles.

'My goodness, it's not booming,' replied Mrs. Blue. 'But one must know how to be happy with what one has, don't you think?'

★ ★ ★

When he returned to the kitchen after having taken Mrs. Cérisolles as far as the street, Red Hands noticed that the pig's blood had caught.

'I wasn't careful, I'm not used to gas. This is not going to be edible now.'

Mrs. Blue was sitting down, looking at him with hatred.

'The three weeks that I've spent in Paris have cost me a great deal,' said Red Hands. 'You could have spared me the expense in telling me everything from the first day.'

'By telling you what?'

'That you had buried Colibri in your cellar.'

'Are you mad?'

He sighed. 'And I who hoped that you'd be reasonable! Yesterday, I brought an Indo-Chinese girl here to carry out an experiment. On seeing her, your brother and René both thought I had found Colibri. Proof that they believed she was still alive! While you, you said "Who's she?" because you knew that it couldn't be Colibri. Why not? Because you knew she was dead!'

'You believe I killed Colibri?'

'I never said that. I'm saying that you had buried her, that's different. You wouldn't think so to look at me but I've buried any number of people, and yet I've never killed anyone!'

He tasted the pig's blood; it was certainly inedible.

'It's René Fouques who killed Colibri,' he said.

Mrs. Blue jumped.

'René? ...'

'Well yes. Your "dear" René... it's a sad story, a loathsome tale and I'd prefer not having to talk about it.'

He told her of his talk with Hippolyte Blue in the building in the rue Du Dragon, the trafficking her brother had been involved in via the Titmouse Agency, and the information he had extracted from him – René had seduced Colibri.

'René!' she cried out again.

'But yes. Your "dear" René'.

Now he told her of his trip to rue Ravignan, and René's cynical plans to leave for South America, after having of course sold up the exquisite studio furnished by Mrs. Blue. Finally, the admission of the musician – a pregnant Colibri.

'Four months pregnant. And can you believe what your "dear" René did? He politely showed her the door, explaining to her that he lacked the vocation of a family man. This child, alone in Paris, helpless, completely lost. "It was three days after that she disappeared" René said to me. Three days... It's not difficult to imagine. She read an advertisement on the last page of a newspaper... MIDWIFE... Imagine the type! She hesitated for two days, the poor kid ... and on the third she went there. And she came back to die here. That's it, isn't it?'

'René!' murmured Mrs. Blue.

Her wonderful fluttering hands were like stone figures in her lap. In a voice that sounded almost drowsy she spoke:

'That night, my brother and son were away. In the middle of the night, Colibri dragged herself as far as my room. She was as white as a sheet. An apalling haemorrhage...

She was dying. I carried her on to her bed in the Marys' dormitory where she slept alone. She had been appallingly cut about but she gritted her teeth so as not to cry out. She asked my pardon for the trouble she was giving me.'

'A worthy girl!' Red Hands said.

'She didn't want to tell the name of the man, nor that of the abortionist. She died almost immediately. I didn't even have time to call the Emergency Services. Afterwards, I told myself that if the police come, they will accuse me. I took her down to the cellar.'

There was silence, then Red Hands carried on :

'When I came here, you thought that I knew more than I appeared to know. That it was really becoming too dangerous to keep the skeleton at your home. One night your brother surprised you in the middle of digging. And as he knew nothing of the Colibri business, and had got it into his head that Cérisolles had killed his wife, you were obliged to take his view, appearing to believe it as well.'

'What are you considering doing?' asked Mrs. Blue, 'going to the police?'

'Do I look like an informer?' grumbled Red Hands.

And in any case, there had not been a crime! There had not been an actual crime. One could not even find in this affair any of that unsavoury bravado that goes with a crime. An act of cowardice? Nothing but a piece of cowardice!

Worse than crime.

Mrs. Blue and Red Hands had spoken hurriedly in low voices. They were like two gravediggers, throwing back earth in rapid shovelfuls to fill in a grave desecrated by an evil-smelling animal.

Presently, a name slipped painfully from Mrs. Blue's lips – 'René... René...'

She rose briskly; she had just heard a furtive noise from the direction of the pantry.

'Hippolyte!'

Fiddling with his beard, Hippolyte came forward with the look of a scared child. He had heard everything

'You were chatting?'

With full force, the marvellous white hand of Mrs. Blue landed on his face.

'Ah, you wanted to play the bachelor. I'm getting rid of this taste of yours for playing the bachelor!'

The slaps rained down heavily. Mr. Blue, huddled between the wall and a sideboard, covered himself with folded arms, moaning:

'Agatha! ... Agatha!'

'Ah! You wanted to play the bachelor! ... Ah! you wanted to play the bachelor...'

Shouts coming from the first floor put an end to this correctional punishment.

'Exactly!' Agnès was screaming on the landing by Gérard's bedroom.

'Aimée is sleeping with René! René has had her! Her, like the others, like Angèle, like Simone, like me, like all of them that he wanted!'

Gérard's voice, outraged: 'Filthy little thing! You're nothing but a little obscenity!'

Agnès was running down the staircase, Gérard behind her, also running. Agnès, on the edge of a fit of hysterics, was shouting:

'René has had no trouble having her. It's she who went to look for him, who ran after him. Ah! She's made a right fool of you, "your" Aimée.'

Everyone, including the three Martha's, met up at the foot of the staircase.

'At this very moment', shrieked Agnès, 'Aimée is at Renés place. In his bed.'

A nervous fit threw her onto the floorboards in convulsions, revealing her miserable thighs that no man had desired – not even René. He had taken her without warmth, ardour, or any other pleasure except that of despoiling. Mrs. Blue and Red Hands carried her on to her bed. Hippolyte followed, looking like a ghost beaten to exhaustion.

'I don't understand,' he stammered. 'If Cérisolles has not killed his wife there is no reason either for him to have killed Maertens, Jeanne Roussignac, Gallant, Bertrand... then who has killed them?'

'But no-one,' Red Hands spoke, wearily.

'No-one!'

Maertens had *actually* been run over by a lorry. Jeanne Roussignac had *actually* been asphyxiated by her stove. Gallant had *actually* been the victim of unknown assailants. Berthault had *actually* become insane and Bertrand had *actually* hung himself because he had cancer.

A black list – the fault of bad luck.

'Sort yourselves out for dinner and put yourselves to bed,' Mrs. Blue commanded the three Marthas in a tone such that they were off in a flash.

She clenched her fists.

'René!' she murmured.

No-one paid attention to the brief noise of an engine in the street – Gérard, who was charging along on a motor bike and sidecar.

Red Hands went out with Mrs. Blue, resolved not to let her go, to prevent her at all costs from causing a disaster. She slammed the door so violently that one of the nails, fixing a sign with the inscription *Protection of the Young Woman* to the pediment, came out of the wall. The notice swung on its remaining nail and stayed vertical – like a flag at half mast.

In the kitchen a cat, up on the sink, was revelling in the pig's blood prepared by the Goupi recipe.

★ ★ ★

Mrs. Blue and Red Hands had been lucky in finding immediately a cruising taxi in the avenue La Motte – Picquet. They went into the building in rue Ravignan without noticing Gérard's sidecar parked some steps away against the kerb.

Red Hands preferred to use the stairs while Mrs. Blue took the lift.

Between floors the lift was enclosed on four sides by four stone walls. Only at landings did one have a view of the staircase. So that Mrs. Blue, going up to the top floor, did not see René de Fouques, who was hurtling down the steps after rushing like a madman out of his studio. No more would Red Hands have seen him if he had not walked up.

'An appalling drama!' the musician cried out. 'Gérard's just found Aimée in my place. He made a terrible scene. The foolish girl was frightened and fired two bullets into his chest. I'm running to find a doctor and to warn the police.'

Thoughts pass rapidly, even through the slow and tranquil mind of a countryman.

'So hang on a moment,' said Red Hands, barring his way. 'It really surprises me that Aimée has shot the lad . She loved him... and for a start she didn't have a gun!'

'She took mine.'

René tried to move down, but the other man, with his heavy build, blocked the way.

'She took your revolver? So you told her where it was? You have unusual conversations for a Don Juan.'

'For goodness sake, let me through,' René shouted, beside himself.

'Don't be in such a rush! You're going to think me stupid but it seems odd to me that you have just left the murderer and her victim like this, by themselves, having a chat. That's hardly wise!'

'I'm telling you that Gérard is dying... get out of the way! A doctor's needed, quickly!...'

'Exactly!' said Red Hands, wedging him against the bannisters and holding him firmly by his jacket. 'It's still a strange thing that you're going on foot to look for the doctor and the police while there's a telephone in your own place. It's so much quicker, the telephone! If you were even an honest farmer, if you were "coming from the Danube" I would understand. But you know how to use the telephone.'

With a violent effort, René tore himself away from

Red Hand's grip and, giving up the idea of going down, climbed the stairs with quick jumps. He reckoned on slipping through the corridors of the maid's quarters and the service stairs at the top of the building.

But reaching the upper landing he stopped, knocked for six. Suddenly his face became greyish, an abject fear contorted him.

He had just caught sight of Mrs. Blue who was coming down in great haste. He leaned his back to the wall, shivering. Normally thin, he seemed to shrink even more.

Red Hands was coming up. Mrs. Blue was coming down.

Between them, René threw glances on all sides, like a panicked animal, searching for an escape.

But there was no other way out except the lift cage – twenty-five yards of empty space...

'Don't let him go through,' Mrs. Blue shouted, 'he has just killed my son!'

'Of course!' Red Hands said, ' I really suspected that it was he who did it!'

★ ★ ★

Stretched out on a rug in the studio Gérard was dying, in the arms of Aimée.

A little earlier, when the young man had burst into the room, he had pounced on René. Without a word, he had struck him.

René had broken free. With the time needed to grab his revolver, cowardly as ever, he had fired two shots point-blank into Gérard.

Then, throwing the girl to the floor as she tried to stop him from escaping, he had run off.

When Red Hands and Mrs. Blue went into the studio Aimée, kneeling by Gérard and holding his head, was speaking in bursts broken by sobs.

'I never liked René you know. I despised him; he gave me the creeps... I came to tell him just what I thought of him; to tell him that he had nothing to expect from me...that I must have been crazy coming here and that I could never come again. I couldn't tell him all this at St. Agatha's... I didn't want to make a scandal. I ought to have written to him... but I have not been able to bear the thought that he would have a letter of mine in his hand. That disgusted me! Oh! Why didn't I write that letter, why did I come back? ... It's all my fault... but, you know, what Agnès told you isn't true. René never touched me... Never... Do you believe me? You must believe me!'

'I believe you! Don't wear yourself out, darling,' Gérard murmured, making an effort to smile.

'I will take care of you... You will recover... My love...'

'Of course, I'm going to recover...'

He was quietly gasping.

'Does it hurt a lot?'

'No. I'm feeling nothing!'

In his chest the pain... like the flashing of fixed lightning .

'Believe it or not, Aimée...'

A speck of froth appeared at the corner of Gérard's mouth. To wipe this away, Aimée took a delicate linen handkerchief from his jacket pocket. A piece of paper folded in four fell out.

'Believe it or not', said Gérard, 'but I found an absolutely charming *Joy of the Beyond.*'

In a cemetery a group of child skeletons were dancing in a ring....'

'Don't talk... don't talk, Gérard.'

'I'm fine, don't worry:

So these child skeletons are dancing in a ring. A little way away there is the skull of another child skeleton. Nothing but the skull. Just lying on the ground. He's not watching those who are dancing in a ring; he's looking the other way.'

'Yes, Gérard, I see. So what?'

'Then one of the dancing skeletons says to the other, referring to the skull on the ground "what's that one doing?"'

'"*Leave it*" *the other replies. "He's skulking!*" …That's curiously smashing, don't you find, darling?'

It was on this ultimate '*Joy of the Beyond*' that this daydreamer, this gentle, laughing Bohemiam, this 'wonderful lazybones" as his mother had said, gave his last gasp…

Mrs. Blue leaned back on the door, remaining silent with a fixed look, as still as a statue.

Red Hands lifted Gérard, carried him off in his arms like a child to behind the curtains which made up the bedroom.

Aimée followed him.

Red Hands put Gérard down on the bed, closed his eyes and crossed his hands on his chest. The young man seemed to smile, as though he was continuing to enjoy himself with his last *Joy*, or rather as though, now that he had passed over to the other side, he had just found a really funny tale, at the expense of the living – those comical living beings.

Without even being aware of it, Aimée was still holding the piece of folded paper which had fallen from Gérard's pocket and which she had unconsciously retrieved.

She kept it in the hollow of her hand in a ball which she was squeezing… squeezing… .

Shortly afterwards, when Red Hands returned to the studio, Mrs. Blue was no longer leaning back against the door. She was standing motionless and speechless with the same fixed expression, near an armchair in which René was sitting, or rather slumped.

Red Hands went to her and touched her gently on the shoulder. At this slight contact she almost jumped out of her skin.

Then, with a sleepwalker's step, she moved towards the telephone standing on a pedestal table and dialled a number.

'Hallo, CID? I'm telephoning from the studio of René de Fouques, 11 rue Ravignan. René de Fouques has just killed my son…'

She was speaking in a calm, steady voice.

'And me,' she continued,' I have just killed René de Fouques.'

Red Hands jumped and looked with astonishment at René slumped in the chair.

'Understood,' concluded Mrs. Blue, 'I'm waiting for you...'

She hung up and turned towards Red Hands.

'I strangled him while you were in the bedroom,' she said.

When she had seen that her son was dead, she had grabbed René by the throat and with a single grip had crushed his vertebrae without his being able to make a single cry.

It had all been done in ten seconds. After that, she had tossed the body into the armchair.

'Go quickly,' she said to Red Hands and Aimée. 'The police are going to arrive and it's pointless for you to be involved in this. I won't mention you. I'll take it all on myself.'

Before leaving the studio, Red Hands had to touch René de Fouques to convince himself that René really was dead.

CHAPTER 14

RED HANDS ON THE EIFFEL TOWER

Red Hands did not want to leave Paris without at least having looked at it once from the Eiffel Tower. He went up on foot.

A stranger went up at the same time, someone from that irritating breed of obliging people who, seeing that Red Hands was up from the country and thinking to make himself agreeable, pointed out the places of interest.

'Notre Dame... Sacré Coeur... on the other side, the Panthéon... There, that's the dome of the Invalides... down there, the Bastille...'

But Red Hands was peering a great deal further into the distance.

'Over there,' he said, 'Indo-China!'

The stranger laughed:

'You've got good eyesight!'

Leaning out over the city Red Hands was re-enacting the stages of his investigation among the network of major roads. Boulevard St. Michel, Titmouse Private Post, the numbered post boxes, and the informant with the Judas' face who called himself Mr. Miss...

Rue du Dragon, the attic room with the peephole in the wall, that soured child who fondled her breasts, breasts making even Red Hands lose his head!

The Flea Market, the exotica, the migrating skeleton. Avenue Charles Floquet, the *Charity for the Protection of the Young Woman*, the matrimonial traffic, the cellar of bones...!

Austerlitz, Montparnasse, Saint-Lazare where the fledglings, flown from the provincial nest, landed in the lap of the *Lady of the Stations*.

Rue Boinod, the flat of the mournful and terrified cuckold.

Rue Tiphaine, the Charentes hôtel, swarming with North African immigrants.

Rue Ravignan, the studio scented with Russian Leather....

And – heaven knew where – the premises of the backstreet abortionist.

From the sordid to the sordid, by way of the sordid, that was all that Red Hands could have known of Paris.

'The fault of bad luck!' once again.

For of course there were also the catholic churches, protestant meeting-houses, theatres, fashion houses, libraries, museums, beautiful shops, beautiful hospitals and maternity homes. Not to mention the Salvation Army, although Red Hands had known it only as symbolised by Hippolyte Blue – still the fault of bad luck.

'It's beautiful, eh?' The chatterbox spoke.

'In the past, really ages ago,' said Red Hands, 'there wasn't a single house here, nor one human being. Just the river, the forest and wild animals. It will come back! All this will crumble into ruins. The grass will eat the stones and the ironwork. It will all be covered with creepers, brambles and brushwood. Of course, it will take a great deal of time – but time doesn't count. There will be nothing more than the river, the forest and the animals, as before. The air will be breathable again!'

'Well,' the man mumbled, somewhat uneasy, 'you aren't the fun-loving type, I must say!'

Red Hands raised his hat to him in a large sardonic gesture and headed towards the stairway.

At the foot of the Tower, a street vendor made him offers:

'Guide to Paris and its surroundings... plan of Paris...

map of the Métro... bus routes ... souvenir album of views of Paris in pocket or postcard size. Also, I have fountain pens with a panoramic view of Paris inlaid down the handle... the Eiffel Tower in miniature... Also, I have,' he slipped into a sudden confidential tone, half unfolding a sort of accordion of photographs, 'also, I have some special photographs... Pleasures of Paris.'

Red Hands raised his hat grandly to him, irritated.

He was going back to the rivers, forests and animals of Goupi country!

★ ★ ★

He did not leave alone.

He took Aimée and the three Marthas. Agnès had packed her bags and cleared off in some unknown direction.

Red Hands was returning the four young ladies to the rivers, the forests, and the animals of their own region that they would have been better never to have left.

He would take Aimée to her father and would explain and arrange things. He was no great shakes at speeches but, what is better, he knew how to speak to people in a way they understood – straightforwardly and with humanity.

This tour through the provinces was going to be a pleasant trip, and rather expensive; his wallet would be flat. Never mind! Red Hands and money... Anyway, in the event of need the Goupis were there – Shilling, Law, Adage, Monsieur. He would always be able to do a little blackmail with them – with respect to the treasure!

And then, what? Rescuing four rather silly girls who'd got off to a bad start; that would be worth the trouble and the expense!

Red Hands had come too late to save Mousmé. At least he would have saved what he could!

From his investigation he brought back only a yellowed

and creased photograph, the sad and somewhat distant profile of a beautiful young lady on a postage stamp, together with twenty-seven bones which, suitably arranged, made up the hand of a corpse.

And poor Aimée, overcome with grief, opposite Red Hands in the compartment, what she was bringing back in returning to the country was also a death – in her heart the name and the image of a dead man.

Gérard... All that Paris had succeeded in giving her as a gift.

No, let's be fair. She had loved and she had been loved...

And for that reason, living no longer seemed to her very desirable.

After the stop at St. Pierre-des-Corps, Red Hands was not immediately aware of the absence of Aimée as the express was setting off again. But from the platform where she had got down, the young lady knocked on the glass.

It was only to bid him farewell.

'Quick! Quick, get back in! he shouted.

She shook her head.

'Goodbye, Red Hands! Tell my father not to worry about me. Where I'm going I'll not have need of anything any longer – ever. Tell him I love him with all my strength. Tell him that I kiss him and that I ask his forgiveness.'

'Well then,' thought Red Hands. 'This idiot is going to throw herself into the water, or under a train!'

He shouted, 'Get in Aimée. Don't be stupid. Get in for God's sake!'

But, increasing her steps to keep pace with the train, she replied:

'Tell my father I'm going to write to him.'

She ran on, out of breath.

Some stupid burks leaning out of the carriage doors laughed; this seemed comical to them!

'Tell my father I'll pray for him. I'm going to Lisieux,

to the convent. The Carmelite convent,' she shouted with all her strength for the train was rumbling as it picked up speed.

She stopped, dropped her suitcase and blew a kiss to poor Red Hands – her last secular gesture.

And there was nothing left on the platform but a big child, sobbing.

★ ★ ★

In the rue Du Carmel in Lisieux, in front of the convent door, Aimée opened her handbag. She took out the piece of paper, folded in four, which had fallen from Gérard's pocket in the studio in rue Ravignan. It carried a few lines in pencil which she knew by heart but wanted to read again:

A cemetery. Child skeletons dancing in a ring. Some way away the skull of a child skeleton lying on the ground. They saw only the nape of his neck. One child: 'What's that one doing?' Another: 'Leave it! He's skulking!'

With passion Aimée pressed this relic to her lips.

This touching testament of Gérard, would she have the heart to tear it up? Yes, it had to be. It was the moment of absolute renunciation. She tore the paper and offered up the pieces to the breeze.

She raised and let fall the knocker of the convent door. A sister came to open it. The same sister who, once already, before the trip to Paris, had opened it and asked :

'What can I do for you, Miss?'

And Aimée had burst out laughing in the face of this nun who so strangely looked like her. Then, she had run away

'What can I do for you, Miss?' The nun asked.

Aimée had prepared a lengthy statement.

'Sister, I have come to seek the grace of being admitted among you, so as to dedicate myself to the service of God.'

But what she said was much more straightforward.

'Sister... Oh! Sister...' Her voice broke and once again, tears choked her.

'Let me come in. Keep me... Keep me...'

The nun touched Aimée lightly on the shoulder with a translucent hand.

'Come, my sister. I'm going to take you to our Mother.'

And the tall door shut again silently.

★ ★ ★

The shadows of dusk lengthened over the plain.

Red Hands went on with long strides over Goupi land. Red Hands, who did not own a square inch of the ground.

He was happy.

In this landscape everything spoke to him in a familiar tongue.

The darkness was well able to veil the details; he knew them all, he could place them accurately. He could name all these fires, these peaceful homes where the solid blokes trudged around with their pocket knives, clogs and caps.

Yes, indeed, with his own cap stuck firmly on his head, holding the wicker basket in one hand and the solemn opera hat in its paper bag in the other, Red Hands was happy. Suffocation was giving way to breathing.

Not that sadness and pain had no hold on his heart; they were tracing their furrows in it, attacking and mauling it. Just as the ants, the woodlice, the whole pack of boring insects, of gnawing creepies, attack the bark of an old oak and perforate it with fissures and channels. But with all its mass and its girth, its thousand serpentine roots and its hundred thousand leaves, the giant plant still enjoys its sap and its life.

And so, bleed as it might, the old peasant heart of Red Hands carried on beating with the rhythm of unstoppable joy.

At Poste Manquée station, Red Hands had settled the three Marthas for the night with the inn-keeper Fonchéramp, a citizen who would never set the Thames on fire, thank God, but a friend, a good fellow – a fool but a golden fool. It was a far more dependable safety than '*The Protection of the Young Woman…*'.

Red Hands passed by Goupi-Monsieur's place to get back his dog Satan. He was invited to supper. He had wanted to turn the invitation down, he really was in a hurry to get back to his hut in the forest, but there are certain things which are not done.

While the servant was cutting bread for the soup, the others all observed him with a keen curiosity. Law, Adage, Shilling, Gazette, Monsieur, Lily… This suit, this wicker basket, this paper bag. What kind of trip was Red Hands returning from? Of course, they did not ask him, that would not have been proper; there are certain things which are not done.

And he was in no hurry to tell them.

Paris was a long way away. Here, there was neither telephone nor lift. He was not among the frenzied, but with people to whom the land each day teaches the virtues of patience, and that what gives a good flavour to things is often the time they take to mature. For instance, if grapes ripened in a week, would one have as much pleasure in drinking the wine?

It was only after the final mouthful, the last glass of wine, the last pocket knife closed, after the final handshake, and when already he was on the threshold that Red Hands turned and announced in his placid normal voice:

'Incidentally, I did not tell you. I've just spent three weeks in Paris. I made an investigation. I'll tell you about this but, for the moment, I'm going to bed.'

'Alright. Come for lunch whenever you want, and you can tell us.'

Only one of them was impatient to know, like a cat on hot bricks. Goupi-Monsieur. Inevitably. He had himself lived in Paris and was still not totally detoxicated.

★ ★ ★

Red Hands was plodding through the undergrowth. With hand in jacket pocket he was rolling between his fingers the knuckle bones – all he had brought back from the capital.

One hand. A right hand.

He recalled the tiny hand of Mousmé as a child, picking blackberries in the hedges, stroking the flanks of Alberte the mare, of Satan the dog, and playing with Red Hand's magical dolls. The hand of Mousmé the schoolgirl, drawing lines on a slate or, what is far greater fun, with a piece of charcoal on sandstone. The hand of Mousmé, the young lady, quick to push away the exploring fingers of the bold and to box the ears of the insolent. Finally, the hand of Mousmé which had written the farewell letter to Red Hands : *Forgive me. I'm really fond of you. But I have no choice other than to leave. I will come back – one day.*

He stopped abruptly as he came in sight of his hut. There was a light there! Oddly, instead of baring his teeth and growling, Satan dashed off like an arrow towards the shack. A second later he emerged with yelps of delight.

A graceful figure appeared. A sing-song voice that Red Hands knew well cried out happily:

'Uncle Red Hands! ... Uncle Red Hands!'

★ ★ ★

'You see,' said Mousmé, 'in the letter that I left you, I promised you that I would come back one day. I've come back!'

Paris – she had never gone there! She had been spared the sad privilege of knowing St. Agatha's, the moustached Mrs. Blue and Hippolyte the bearded Lady of the Stations.

She had gone to Marseilles. There she had joined up with a wealthy compatriot. And he had .... well, quite simply taken her off to Indo-China. In this way she had been able to know the country of her birth, which she had left when very young. It was there that she had passed the last three years, a happy existence without dramas, upsets nor complications.

Why had she not written?

What a question! The Tongkings never send letters.

She had come back to spend three months in France. Then she would set off again for Hanoi where she would go and join her lover again. They would be married.

Life was a real fairy tale!

'Well! So much the better!' Red Hands replied. 'But I've just come back from a family dinner. How is it that none of these wretched Goupis has told me that you were back in this country?'

'I got back this morning,' said Mousmé, 'and I waited for you here. Do you think I wanted to see anyone before you?' She eyed the hat, the wicker basket and the dark suit. 'You are back from a trip?'

''Errh,' Red Hands was evasive, 'I had to go to a funeral.'

But in reality...

Colibri?

Colibri and Mousmé were not the same person. There was a Mousmé and there had been a Colibri.

For three weeks on end Red Hands, believing his investigation was about his great niece Mousmé, Tongking's daughter, had actually investigated...

Ah well, yes, there had been a mix-up.

The old snapshot, creased and yellowed, was that of Colibri, Indo-Chinese like Mousmé.

'They all look alike,' Gérard Blue used to say, 'like sparrows...'

Poor little Colibri.

With his mind blank Red Hands watched Mousmé's fingers playing with the formal old opera hat. Those living fingers.

He came out of the hut and in four strides came up to the well that they called the well of Goupi-Dead since she had drowned herself in it, because of an unhappy love affair.

The one who used to be called Goupi-Belle when alive. He plunged his hand into his pocket, pulled out the fistful of bones and dropped them into the water.

He then went back to the hut.

'What's wrong with your hand?' asked Mousmé.

The stones and the coping of the well were overgrown, encumbered and carpeted with a thick spider's web of brambles. Its thorns had scratched his flesh.

Red Hands had blood on his hand.

THE END